LIVING AMONG STRANGERS

For Karen, Thank you for Reading this!

LIVING AMONG STRANGERS

A Collection of Short Stories by

RICHARD SCHMITT

Richard Schmitt
WVWC 2018

Adelaide Books
New York/ Lisbon

2017

Living Among Strangers
A Collection of Short Stories
By Richard Schmitt

Copyright © 2017 By Richard Schmitt

Published by Adelaide Books, New York / Lisbon
An imprint of the Istina Group DBA
adelaidebooks.org

Editor-in-Chief
Stevan V. Nikolic

All rights reserved. No part of this book may be reproduced in any manner whatsoever without written permission from the author except in the case of brief quotations embodied in critical articles and reviews.

For any information, please address Adelaide Books
at info@adelaidebooks.org

ISBN13: 978-0-9995164-2-3
ISBN10: 0-9995164-2-6

Printed in the United States of America

For Brother John

Contents

- *11*   FLASHPOINT
- *23*   CONFIRMATION
- *42*   NUN BLOOD
- *55*   SKIN TIGHT
- *67*   THE TRESTLE
- *87*   LEAVING VENICE
- *103*   WINTER
- *110*   MOTION SICKNESS
- *129*   STILL LIFE
- *138*   INTERNAL INJURIES
- *155*   THE HEARTBREAK BUSINESS
- *175*   BECAUSE WE ARE HUMAN
- *191*   UNTIL THE MORNING COMES
- *197*   LIVING AMONG STRANGERS
- *217*   BREATHING
- *233*   About the Author

Acknowledgements

These stories have originally appeared in the following magazines and publications:

Flashpoint in *Blackbird Literary Journal*, Fall 2007

Because We Are Human in *Southern Humanities Review*, Winter 2014

Skin Tight, in *Cimarron Review* Spring 2011

Nun Blood in *Gulf Coast* Fall 2007

Leaving Venice in *Mississippi Review / New Stories of the South:* Year's Best 1997.

Motion Sickness *Adelaide Literary Magazine*, September 2017

Still Life *Trillium*, 2013

Until the Morning Comes *Still / 34th Parallel* #40

Living Among Strangers *Sequestrum* winter 2017

Breathing *Shenandoah*, Winter 2016.

Flashpoint

No weapons—No Bibles! Words from a security man at the checkpoint we filed through approaching the Temple Mount, the place where Jesus spoke, where walls came tumbling down, where all those conflicting temples are, were, or will be, where we can't do shit according to this blustering soldier, a boy really, given a uniform and a godless machinegun. No weapons—No Bibles! That's what he said, and that's how I felt, no religion and nothing with which to fight.

    I'd already gotten into it, a fight I mean, that morning with my girlfriend, Iris—a wonder like the flowering plant, the Greek rainbow goddess, and, oh yes, the beautiful part of our eyes. I'd lost her somewhere in the confusion of the checkpoint. No proselytizing, preaching, postulating, lecturing, sermonizing, moralizing. No nuns or priests, as least none dressed like nuns or priests. Israeli security forces can tell. Something in the eyes, the saintly expressions, the secret smiles while conspiring with The Lord. That can't be faked. I was hoping to be overlooked, a pothead student, a possible divinity prospect on a summer trip that was supposed to cement my everlasting salvation, or at least shoe-in the next two years of grad school. The trip ended up having the opposite effect. I was thinking of dropping college. I had my four years in. My mother was the mayor of a small town back home, my father the chief of police; they'd never even gone to college. Why not mount a political career? No didacticism, agitation, heckling, mocking, taunting, ranting or raving. Nothing on your body: No icons, symbols, amulets, voodoo dolls, juju beads, scapulars or other sanctified scrap metal. No right or wrong carried within—the boy soldiers will know. I fingered my pot, two buds in a film canister. No photos, renderings, artist sketches, illustrations. You leave with nothing when you come here. The checkpoint was a steel structure, metal detector, bulletproof chute to the holy hill. I was hazy on the whole weight of the place, the relevant reverence, holiness, significance. But that's why we came, to check it out, to be in the know about holy spots, places bearing on our lives, places where things come together and fall apart. What made the walls tumble? Did they fall from neglect? Random chance? Divine wrath? No questions or answers—grim looks and long lines only.

Through the checkpoint we were funneled into a narrow overheated walkway, fenced and railed. I'd had it with being jammed in the kneecap by the umbrella of a fat lady in front of me so I pinched her butt quick and moved to one side as she whirled setting off a chain reaction where three or four people were whacked with the umbrella which she wasn't supposed to have because umbrellas were, apparently for good reason, not allowed.

I am not prone to rash pinching but that morning Iris told me she missed her period which had set off another kind of chain reaction, panic, denial, anger, despair. How could that happen? I demanded answers as if I were not involved. We were careful. Apparently not, she said. Right after school got out we were back home messing around on Bare Butte, naked college kids clamoring all over the mountain, upsetting the Indians: Nowah'wus to the Cheyenne, Mato Paha to the Lakota, Bare Butt to the drunken bikers. Expansive momentous vistas, expansion to hitherto untapped markets, legs wide open, grit in the cracks. The grade-A #1 synthetic contraceptive sheath device that cost me seventy-five cents in a Mount Rushmore restroom snapped like a career postal worker. Had to be intervention, an act of God, or too much grit. My divine future looked bleak. I was seeped in holiness, damn it. The lady with the umbrella screamed feminist rhetoric which was—goes without saying—not allowed. She was ejected by soldiers in full combat regalia, Uzis, hard boots, plastic wrist restraints, all very much allowed to prevent uprisings. She bellowed all the way to the exit gate. No Temple Mount for her. Or mount to the temple—it was a wooden walkway, elevated and enclosed with wire mesh like a tube so one couldn't divert from the path, the chosen way—diversion, digression, deviation were not allowed.

Someone asked: Is this the way Jesus walked? I duck-walked like Charlie Chaplin and said, Jesus walked like this. A soldier pointed his Uzi at me. No funny walking. I was trying to lighten up, lighten my load, I was feeling guilty about the fight with Iris. I wiped sweat from my brow and looked for her back down the line. Looking back can be dangerous. People get nervous. Have second thoughts. Reconsider situations. The walkway was tight, the heat intense, we were packed in like cattle, like lambs to slaughter. Jews are jumpy about lines in general, about herds, about cattle cars. Most of these were American Jews, tourists. There was a group of Christians from Kansas—incognito because groups were not allowed—all wearing the same rip-off holy shoes, sandals like Jesus wore sold by Arab vendors. Made in China. When I looked back people stared at me. I was taller and looked down on them. I made a shocked face as if something bad was happening behind them. They ducked without pause. Two of them hit the deck causing panic and chaos up and down the line, a chain reaction again, cause and effect. I walked on, uninvolved, unattached.

But I was attached. A missed period was perilous because we attended a major Catholic University where I had a major grad-school assistantship, and, Iris's Dad was a major force on the Board of Trustees. We were supposed to be holy. Iris never traveled without her sacred-heart Jesus photo pinned damply to her underwear. On the body, (not allowed), a hidden bust and blood, inviolable deity near the source of life. Christ in cunt to put it crudely. He's a musty old relic anyway. Strung out on a cross on Friday, holed up for the weekend, in need of a lift by Sunday. So what the smell. Holiness comes with a price. Stinky, soggy, slick Lord-on-a-card in her crotch, laminated for protection—can't be too careful, can't trust anyone, especially someone tricky with loaves and fishes, especially someone with a cross to bear—had to have an agenda (not allowed), especially someone nailed to a cross—had to hold a grudge (grudges are allowed, hence the tight security). Iris wasn't even on the pill. Totally irresponsible.

She must have been detained at the checkpoint, strip-searched, soiled, felt up by soldiers because they'd see she was hiding something, because she was hot, they'd run her through a pregnancy detector, a good Catholic girl from Notre Dame for Christ's sake. Or not. She might have carried the picture just to break the rules. Carrying a baby she'd already broken the rules—no pregnant girls at Notre Dame. Her parents thought she was a virgin. They didn't even know she smoked cigarettes, and here she was, climbing Temple Mount with contraband. We could be whipped, flogged, stoned. Well, we were a bit of that already, indulging on the hotel balcony after breakfast, after the fight. That's another thing we do—dope, we smoke it. She carried that too, in her underwear with everything else.

Up the hill we trudged with bare feet in chains and clawing at flies and rabid dogs—whoa that can't be right, that's just how it felt, a hot day, sticky with sweat, and this baby burden like a grist wheel around my neck, our necks. Iris was in as much trouble as me, more maybe, she'd have to carry the physical burden, and the stain of sin. We hadn't meant to fight, didn't want to ruin the trip, we tried to talk rationally, discuss options. Marriage? Abortion? Suicide? Martyrdom? Iris was raised by nuns, well, her parents weren't nuns but they might as well have been. They made her go to church daily. Daily! Bare knees below plaid skirts, the grain of wooden prayer rails embedded. She had nuns for teachers from grade one, her older sister was a missionary in Africa, one of those that wears white and isn't afraid of leprosy. Crazy Catholics.

Iris was devout but got horny in dangerous places. The supermarket (very bright), the library (very quiet), Church (very holy), her parent's house (the walls had ears), Temple Mount (not allowed). Where was she? Her parents were Catholic-charity-giving patrons that would disown her in a heartbeat if one sounded in her belly. They financed this summer trip. Do you good, they said, to see some holy sites. They trusted me because I had a ticket to divinity school. Because I am tall and apparently well-mannered. They didn't know I wanted to scrap religion for politics, run for office, or just run. They didn't know I screwed their daughter in dangerous places. All summer long we'd done the sodden deed at religious sites: Lumbini, (birthplace of Buddha), Lhasa, (home of Dalai Lama), Thebes, (free camel rides), Rome, (an orgy of Catholics), Canterbury, (tails), Lourdes, (blessed virgins and Viagra water), Turin, (holy headwear). Oracles from Delphi to Redwood City, we did them all. Pilgrimages to Mecca, Vrindavan Mashhad, Al-Haram al-Sharif. Shimmering Jesus, at the top of the Mount what a sight, site, whatever. Is there a golder dome in the world? It was more impressive than St. Patty's Cathedral. But hold on: Paint! For Christ's sake, maybe Mohammad's sake, in any case the Dome of the Rock when we finally got up to it was hung with scaffolding. Workers splattered with gold paint sat munching pita bread out of red and white mini-coolers, one of them had a chrome Starbucks mug. There was muttering from the pilgrims. This would ruin our holy photos.

The line dispersed into chaos at the top, people drifted about irreverently, stomping on sacred ground. I looked back wondering where the hell Iris was. I wanted to tell her all would be well. I'd smooth things over. Stand by her. I wandered aimless among ruins and remains of ruins. There was the foundation of the first temple, maybe. Nothing was certain except the soldiers, the smell of gun oil, and the bomb-disposal units resembling underwater diving bells. There were beggars of course, mandatory at a place like this, a blind boy in rags with his palm out, off to one side his connections, promoters, maybe parents, conspicuous in black robes. What is that stuff they wear? In this heat? Holy Roller clothes? Prayer shawls and checkered headdresses, veils and masks. Halloween on hallowed ground? Hollow more likely, like my divine intentions.

There she was. Ahead of me on the stone steps leading to the mosque, her curly blonde head bobbed among the crowd. Like me she was tall, a volleyball player, long legs and small tits. Did they look bigger? Was she swelling up? I moved toward her through the crowd. She wore a white tank top and shorts, very short, indecent, legs like a gazelle, skin translucent like a lampshade, a body from here to eternity which might not be that far off. I tried to reach her but she was striding out and putting distance on me. I took the steps double time to the top, a vast open space paved with ancient stones, and when I thought she could hear me I shouted "Iris!" And that's when I first noticed the big guy with the machinegun. Running and shouting were not allowed. People ducked and shied. The big guy over by the mosque spoke into a Walkie-talkie. "Iris!" She whirled and jumped and timed a perfect landing with her legs around my waist, her arms around my neck, her mouth mashing mine pretty close to chipping a tooth. "You lost me," I said.

"I hope not," she said. She was relieved. She sucked my mouth. The morning fight forgotten. She hung on. I supported her with my hands clasped under her butt. She wore a digital camera around her neck, the strap transecting her breasts, sunglasses on her head, a map of Jerusalem stuck in her back pocket. People parted around us, averted their eyes, making out was not allowed but we did it anyway, then walked on, hand in hand, an American cliché. Pregnant college students for Christ's sake, seeing the dome of the rock, the gold-domed mosque with tile work like tracks of wild animals. We walked up close and stared. Iris read from a brochure. "It's a sanctuary for a rock," she said. "A womb for a living belief."

I looked at her—I couldn't help myself. "Everything is a womb now."

She didn't take it wrong. "Yes! My body is a temple."

So we were being facetious—or not. "No tumbling down," I said. "We are stone."

"Immaculate."

We stopped to kiss. The sun cooked the tops of our heads. We didn't have the sense to wear hats, we were sticky in white clothes, not all white, that might be construed as a statement and statements were not allowed. All white was incendiary. The color of innocence, and also explosion. That was us: innocence to explosion. "I love you," I said. "I want to marry you and have this baby."

I'd made her happy. But we knew it wasn't that simple. It was like in politics when two parties agree in principle but the practical application is beyond them. We strolled arm in arm under the scaffolding with the painters slapping on the gold and eyeballing us.

"My parent's just redecorated my bedroom," she said. "Pink wallpaper and white carpeting. What the hell am I supposed to tell them?"

"Tell them it was divine intervention." She laughed and we were on to something. "Really," I said. "We'll marry at one of these holy sites." I was serious. We'd say it was a euphoric experience. We'd cite Revelation, an act of God, brought on by the holy trip—it was their idea. And if a baby arrived in eight months—they would be counting—well, that too must be an act of God. Iris held my face to hers and mixed sweat with tears. We were on to something.

We walked around to the front of the mosque. The big guy with the machinegun watched. He lorded over an array of shoes lined up outside the entrance. Leather sandals (rip off holy shoes), rubber flip-flops, a few shiny Italian loafers, white American sneakers (that's what we wore)—Arab women favored stiff black brogans worn without socks. We figured to off our shoes and head in to view the holy rock. We needed the cool inside after the heated decision. But as we approached the big guy, moustache and black turtleneck, blocked our way. He eyeballed Iris up and down: legs, tits, hair, legs again. I tried to steer her around him but he stepped into our path. He was stout but I was tall. He shook his finger at us. "You two no." Strapped to his shoulder was a big black Russian Kalashnikov rifle. On his belt the walkie-talkie and a clip full of cartridges. "You no go in," he said.

"We're not Jewish," I said.

"But you could be."

I considered this. We could be anything. But right then we were hot, we were frying in the sun, and determined to go inside where it was dark and cool and safe in the sanctuary around the rock. "We're American," I said, trying to be reasonable. "We're going to be married."

"Not here," he said. "You no go."

I don't know what his problem was, maybe he knew we were hiding something. "We're people of good faith," I said. I gestured toward Iris. Was the guy blind? Look at this world wonder. He studied her crotch where the V of her white shorts came together. Old Arab women and young girls stared at us with contempt. Iris with her shorts and wild hair and me peach-faced in the harsh sun. We seemed very white among the black robes and dusty shoes and the heat seeping out of the stones. "Look man," I brought up my finger for emphasis. The guy turned his back on us. "Hey, I'm talking to you!"

Iris grabbed my arm. "Forget it," she said. "Let's go."

I stopped and looked at her. She was disappointed. "No." I turned to go after the guy. What the hell was his problem? We were going to be married damn it and live happily ever after—didn't he watch movies—we're from Notre Dame, U.S.A. motherfucker. He knew that word. I must have said it out loud because he spun his weapon off his shoulder and there was the black hole of the barrel saying not allowed.

I held my palms out. "Look, we stood in line like everyone else."

He stepped close, the big greasy rifle between us. "You leave now."

Iris griped my arm from behind but I wasn't budging. "We're immovable, Pal, permanent, solid, fixed. We're in for the duration."

Then two things happened at once. Before I could move, Iris swung around my arm as if she was trying to face me. She wanted me to quit the standoff and leave. But the guy must have decided I wasn't going to, which I wasn't, and he swung the butt of the rifle towards my gut catching poor Iris in the stomach. She buckled. I caught her halfway down but I was off balance and we both tumbled onto the dusty stones. Truth is it was more of a glancing blow than a solid gut shot. She barely had the wind knocked out of her. I could tell because she was talking right away, not gasping or breathless. "I'm fine, I'm fine," she said. "Can we just get out of here?"

The guy stood back in the shade, the gun back on his shoulder. He lit a cigarette and lorded over the people approaching the mosque. I rose and reached down to help Iris rise. At first I thought I was seeing things. I looked closer. Iris didn't feel it yet. She must have seen something in my face and she drove her hand into her waistband, down lower, and it came away red. We saw the future clearly defined, a crimson stain, irreconcilable, unable to be taken back, a dark splotch like a wound at the white V between her legs. White, the color of innocence, the color of explosion before cooling flame fries and smoke chokes and blood flows. Hot site here. Flashpoint: a place of irreversible change, like a missed period, like conception, like looking back. We helped each other to the nearest exit gate. We would weep on back to school. We'd say the trip was great. Enlightening. Did us a lot of good. Iris would move into her pink and white room. I'd stick to divinity school slightly askew, go the theology route where I could safely study blameless acts of God. We'd be married in time and have kids and what we lost on the Temple Mount that day would stay between us, driving us closer together and further apart, as we make our way down Via Dolorosa, the way of sorrows.

Confirmation

Phillip Madeira was the kid that made me believe in God. The nuns at St. Joes couldn't do it. Confession, Communion, Confirmation—the holy shebang—none of it stuck until this kid from across the street christened me in God-fearing guilt and solitude. Mad Madeira we called him, called from outside rock-throwing range. He was the neighborhood tantrum kid, a splay-footed wailer of menacing oaths, a crier of elephant tears, a brash tattletale, snitch, rat, squealer, shunned and reviled in our neighborhood, and we—myself and younger brother Butch—did all we could to incite Phil's notorious temper, safely, from, see above, outside rock-throwing range.

One summer day my brother and I and Madeira were in our yard watching my mother dig holes for rose bushes she would plant along the picket fence that ran in front of our new house, a common two-story New England colonial with attached garage, nearly identical to every other house in the neighborhood, all set on quarter-acre lots of Sears-fertilized lawns mowed by Sears-loving dads on Saturday mornings. This was suburbia in the sixties. No sidewalks or traffic except our dads coming and going from work, and in the summer afternoons the ice cream truck, and at dusk the town mosquito sprayer. We rode bikes, played whiffleball, street hockey, and violent games sprung from popular TV shows. I know it was 1960 because I was fondling a brand new penny. My little brother Butch held a whiffleball and a bat. He was tossing the ball to himself and smacking it straight up in the air, watching the erratic flight rise and fall, and when it dropped snaring it with one hand. Our plan was to get a game up without including Phillip Madeira who was lusting after my shiny new penny. He said he wanted it because he was a coin collector—Madeira claimed to be everything. Said he had every year but the current one. "Every year?" I said. "Since the beginning of time?"

"Since 1909," Phil said. "The first year they made pennies."

Madeira always stated things as if they were indisputable facts, but often we felt he was full of crap. "Is that true Mom?" I asked my mother.

"I really don't know, sweetheart." She wore flowered gardening gloves to handle the thorny rose bushes.

"It's true," Madeira said. "Before that they had Indian-heads."

Madeira's dog was named Penny, possibly something to do with this, but I suspected he wanted my new coin simply because he didn't have it and I did and he was a vindictive Protestant who coveted his neighbor's goods which I assumed didn't matter since I thought the Ten Commandments were solely for Catholics. Madeira was the first Protestant we'd ever met. We didn't have them in

South Boston where we lived until I was seven, Butch six. Smack! The whiffleball corkscrewed up over the lawn, seemed to pause in indecision, then spiraled wildly down until Butch shot out a hand and caught it.

The day we moved to this new neighborhood Mom told us the Madeira family went to a different church. There was a different church? Who knew? Phil and his older brother David attended public school while Butch and I suffered the nuns at St. Joe's. The nuns made it sound as if Protestants were akin to Nazis. Jews even. But they also said Jesus a Jew. It was puzzling. When Jesus said love your neighbor did he mean all our neighbors? Even fat-head Madeira, the Protestant? Even more mystifying was the fact that Mr. Madeira, Phil's father, was a Protestant minister. That their spiritual sages had wives and kids and dogs and lived in neighborhoods among normal people stressed to me their deficient salvation system.

My plan was to buy Madeira out of our yard with the penny, because I didn't care about it, I just wanted to play whiffleball. The neighborhood kids weren't allowed near Phil which was why we needed to ditch him to play ball. Butch knew what I was thinking. My little brother and I communicated with smirks and shrugs, a raised eyebrow, a head bob, a fleeting glance, the toss of a flighty whiffleball, so we knew that if Madeira thought we were trying to ditch him he'd fly into a rage and start roaring and wagging his giant head. The head of Madeira was hard and heavy like a medicine ball, and so big he had gaps between his teeth like a jack-o-lantern. His older brother, David, told us Phil was forced to wear a football helmet until age five because when he threw a tantrum he'd pound the house with his head. The floors, walls, furniture, appliances, the family car, all had dings and dents from Phil's plummeting head. He'd caught me with a few glancing blows, but I was a slippery kid, sneaky, and secretly scared of Mad Madeira.

At some point, while I stood scheming with Butch idly smacking and catching the ball and Madeira still lusting after my shiny new coin, our cat came rocketing across the front yard pursued by two feverish dogs and wedged herself into a defensive spot among the rose bushes while the dogs, clumsy and in their own way, growled and yapped. Madeira hopped up and down shouting, "Sic'em, Penny! Sic'em!" Nothing in our neighborhood sparked more passion than our dogs. Bikes, sports, our parents—these were important but our dogs defined us. My dog Ginger was tawny and thin like a greyhound. In terms of flat-out speed Gin was supreme, and she had nothing against our cat, she was simply riled up by Madeira's dog, Penny, a common border collie who Phil insisted was faster, tougher, smarter, and so on. He'd bring his thunderous head down on anyone who said different.

Like her owner, Penny flew irrational in frenzied situations. With the cat hissing and spitting, Penny snarled and snapped. Mom calmly went about her digging business. The cat fired claws from her rosebush fortress and caught Penny on the nose drawing blood. Blood always raised the stakes. Madeira screamed that he'd sue. Phil often threatened to sue people—we weren't sure what suing was but Mom said Phil got that from his parents. At the sight of Penny's bloody nose Phil charged into the fray, trying to stomp our cat. The dogs dodged and lunged. When Ginger got in Phil's way he drew back his foot and kicked her in the ribs. A solid thump. Another weird thing about Madeira, he didn't go barefoot in the summer like we did, he wore high-top leather brogans, school shoes, with baggy shorts and no socks. And those shoes packed a wallop in Ginger's ribs. That was a mistake.

My little brother was what people call "laidback". Butch was stocky and blonde and nearly as tall as me. The nuns said the name Butch didn't suit him because he wasn't a tough guy or a bully. His real name was Joshua; no one called him that except the nuns if he was in trouble which was never. Butch was a teacher's pet. He clapped erasers, washed the blackboard, was granted bathroom passes without question and, unlike me, was never commanded to the corner for daydreaming. When President Kennedy got after us to become physically fit, Butch could punt, pass and kick, further-faster-bigger-better than kids two years older. In Little League he was star shortstop and home run king. In Cub Scouts Butch tied all the knots before anyone. He made fire with flint and dry leaves, knew which berries to eat, which ivy vines to avoid, how to chop with an ax, catch a fish, tie a tourniquet. Butch earned the tiger-wolf-bear badges pronto, and in just a few years would shoot the Arrow of Light into full-blown Boy Scouts while I languished in Weebelos. Butch was known to react fearlessly in any situation.

When Phillip Madeira kicked our dog in the ribs Butch dropped the ball and bat. I watched him launch himself broad-jump style onto Madeira's back and lock both arms around Phil's head. Madeira roared and whirled, swung his head like an Olympic hammer thrower trying to shake off Butch who twisted the thrashing head back and forth as if to wrench it from its roots. Mom looked up and said, "Boys, boys…" She wasn't upset; she merely wanted to plant her roses. The cat hissed, the dogs growled, Madeira roared, bloody-nose Penny humped Phil's leg. I stood there doing nothing while Butch grimly tried to tear Phil's head off. He wailed so loud his mother came out of their house and started across the street which made my mom take a deep breath and speak more firmly. "Boys, stop it now!"

Phil's mother always wore a dress and had her hair sculpted and sprayed as if she just came from church. She bore down on us. Butch pushed off Phil and sailed free, landing on his feet well out of head-wagging range while Phil stumbled to the ground shedding elephant tears of frustration, his shirt was torn and he had grass stains on his knees. We'd seen this a million times, his mother showed up when Phil was crying and blaming everyone but himself. "It was them. They did it. Their cat scratched Penny." It amazed us that his mother always seemed to accept that Phil was innocent and harmless. She took him in her arms and soothed him out of our yard giving a slight, not particularly favorable nod to my mom.

When they were gone, Mom let out a breath. "Something is wrong with that kid," she said. "Stay away from him."

We did. We shunned Phil as a general rule. But, when we were bored, when the summer dog days dragged on so long we forgot how much we longed for them in May, when we misplaced the idea of ever wearing shoes again, when we forgot that the nuns lay in wait for us after Labor Day, we lay in wait for Phil, with tomatoes.

The rose bushes were in the ground and thriving by the end of summer when Butch and I crouched in the grass behind them and the picket fence that ran along the road in front of our house. We waited for Phillip Madeira to come out of his house across the street. Nestled in the grass next to us were two ripe tomatoes filched from Mrs. Sartelli's garden. Mrs. Sartelli lived next door and regularly gave us chocolates and money for doing nothing. The tomatoes were the perfect throwing size of baseballs. We palmed them gingerly because they were full and bloated with seeds and juice. Soft enough to splat! on contact, but also implode in our hands if we were clumsy and didn't let them fly precisely, with velocity but also sufficient arc so that they didn't spin apart in midair before landing on target, the target being Phil Madeira. Ideally, we pictured tomato bombs dropping from the sky and landing squarely atop Madeira's fat head, like a message from God—*Madeira, you suck.*

Hunkered down behind the roses we watched Phil's brother David play basketball in his driveway with two friends. We knew Phil would come out the side door of his house into the driveway and the basketball players would tell him to get lost, and he'd cross his front yard. All summer he'd been parading up and down the street with a marching-band drum driving everyone nuts and threatening to sue us. We didn't know what a marching band was, St. Joes didn't have one, but if Phil liked it we didn't. Eventually he appeared wearing the drum, a tricorn hat, baggy brown shorts and his nasty brogans. We rose to our knees, tomatoes in hand. The basketball players gave him the finger and Phil started across his front yard beating the drum and whistling. Butch and I were ballplayers, we knew how to throw and judge fly balls. Right away when we hurled the tomatoes we saw Butch's throw was higher than mine. His tomato bomb would drop from the sky close to our target; mine had too much velocity and would hit the house. We also saw, to our horror, too late to take anything back, Phil's mother open the front door of their house and step outside. She wore a white dress.

It was not yet high noon. The sun illuminating the front of Madeira's house seemed to increase the brilliance and clarity of everything including the passage of time. I'm certain I wasn't breathing at that point. Next to me, my little brother was likewise suspended in that fearful moment while we watched the tomatoes sail over the road. It seemed as if, at the very second Phil's mother appeared on her front step, God cranked the sun up a notch. As if He not only saw all, as the nuns insisted, but paid attention to some things more than others.

Butch's tomato dropped from the sky, nicked the front point of Phil's tricorn hat, and banged down hard onto the head of his drum. It was a sound unlike any heard in our neighborhood, a soft ripe tomato bursting on a marching-band drum. My tomato, zinging in too fast, made a predicable thud hitting Mrs. Madeira square in the chest and splattering between her breasts on the snow-white dress. From our vantage point it appeared her heart had exploded from her chest and I had the irrational thought that she would die. Both Phil and his mother opened their mouths but the only sound was the basketball pounding the driveway. It is shocking how calm and slowed-down time seems at the instant catastrophic things happen. And we knew this was catastrophic. The only thing worse than hitting someone's mother with a tomato would be a blasphemous church-related sacrilege for which we would burn everlasting in hell.

We ran. bent over behind the roses we hauled ass along the fence until we reached the end of our yard and ran senselessly into the road figuring if we ran fast enough and didn't look back we'd be invisible and the whole fiasco would disappear. But we weren't invisible, and we did look back, at least Butch did. He was a stride ahead of me, we heard Phil roaring behind us, and I saw Butch's wide-eyed face turn and look back over his shoulder.

Phil was a known rock thrower. Something our parents told us never to do, right up there with talking to strangers, playing with matches, and sticking our heads in plastic bags. Each year some kid was snatched on the way to school, burned in a fire, smothered in a trash bag, or blinded for life by a flying stone, at least that is what they told us. And Phil, of course, was no ballplayer, he couldn't throw at all. Which is why later, when I considered the timing of the thing—Butch running before me and turning his head at the very instant the rock Phil threw over an immense distance hit with pinpoint accuracy—I knew the venture had to have been, like the moment Lot's wife looked back, orchestrated from above.

I didn't see the golf-ball-size stone hit my brother's head. I heard a hollow knock like knuckles on wood and saw the stone bounce to the road. What I saw when I looked at Butch, was a smooth coating of shiny red as if someone had candy-appled my brother's head. He made no sound. He stopped running. He held his hands out in front of him like a blind man and said, "I can't see, I can't see." Well there it is, I thought, he's blinded for life. Phil didn't come running but it seemed as if every mother on the block did, including our mom and Mrs. Madeira in her ruined white dress. Butch kept waving his arms around in the road and saying, "I can't see, I can't see."

None of our moms drove. After our dads went to work there was only one car in the neighborhood, a pristine lime-green Cadillac in Mrs. Sartelli's garage. From somewhere a towel was produced and wrapped around Butch's head like a turban. There was an immense amount of blood and it seemed as if everything else was white: the towel, Mrs. Madeira's dress, Butch's t-shirt, and as he was loaded into the car, the white leather interior of Mrs. Sartelli's Cadillac. My mom, before joining Butch on his trip to the hospital, looked at me severely and pointed a bloodied finger toward our house.

I knew when Dad came home I'd get the strap. Punishment was all physical in those days, I wasn't afraid of that. What scared me was confession. Come Saturday I would have to confess this tomato stunt to Father O'Gara. I'd been going to confession since May, Butch not yet. The new routine added a confusing anxiety to my life. Not only did it interfere with Saturday morning cartoons but everything I did was potentially known, exposed, revealed—my deepest secrets condemned and condoned by Father O'Gara on Saturday mornings. We knew at the start of the coming school year Butch would study for his First Confession and I'd be burdened with Confirmation, an even bigger deal than Holy Communion, they said, although they'd previously said Holy Communion was the biggest deal possible, receiving Christ into our bodies via a wafer of bread like a poker chip. We didn't understand any of it. But this new Confirmation thing was so big the nuns said the Bishop had to come do it. When the nuns said "The Bishop" their eyes got huge and they nodded ominously. Sounded as if the Bishop was someone to be avoided, a more imposing figure than Father O'Gara; something I didn't want to think about.

It wasn't until the next day when Mom returned from the hospital that I heard about Butch. I was grounded and couldn't leave my room. Mom came in and sat on the bed. She'd been up all night at the hospital and looked it. She cried easily and often when we misbehaved so that was no surprise. The brain tumor was.

"What's a brain tumor?" I said.

"Very serious," she said quietly.

Throughout the previous 24 hours the plethora of "very serious" situations had piled up. Hitting Mrs. Madeira with the tomato, Phil's miraculous rock, my father's fury—*You're going to pay for that goddamn dress!*—what I was likely to face from Father O'Gara on Saturday. For all I knew I'd be denied Confirmation, not to mention the wrath of God I was sure to suffer on Judgment Day, and now, this mysterious growth in my brother's brain, a sausage-size shadow on the skull X-ray. The astonished doctor's saying very serious to my parents, saying surgery now, no going home, straight to the OR, and no guarantees. Butch may never come home.

In confession to Father O'Gara, I stressed the word Protestant. "I wasn't trying to hit her," I told him, "I was trying to hit this kid. This Protestant kid."

"God made all things," he said. "You throw tomatoes you hurt God. Don't you see that?"

"Yes Father."

But I didn't see. Weren't Protestants the enemy? Didn't they go to a different church?

"Did you apologize to your neighbor?"

"Yes Father."

"You need to apologize to God."

"Yes Father."

"Three Hail Mary's and an Our Father."

I retreated to the prayer rail and fake-prayed until I figured he wasn't watching and I got out of there.

School had started by the time Butch returned from the hospital, his hair shaved, an amazing six-inch scar up the backside of his head which made him a celebrity. The doctors said if the tumor had gone undetected Butch would not have seen teenage years. The stoning by, of all things, a vindictive Protestant, had saved my brother's life. "By the grace of God," the nuns said. We had no clue what grace was. If Butch was a teacher's pet before that summer debacle, he was a miracle child after, a candidate for sainthood, a chosen one. "The Lord works in mysterious ways," the nuns said. At times it seemed as if the nuns were actually praising Phillip Madeira. When by extension of their logic I attempted to point out that if we hadn't thrown the tomatoes, Phil wouldn't have thrown the rock and... About then I'd be cut off with stern looks and admonishments such as "Two wrongs don't make a right, mister." It was puzzling.

In time, Butch's hair grew out and things went back to normal. After school we went to the chapel for communion/confirmation study. We were anxious. Butch was anxious for, I was anxious about. Butch wished ardently for communion because he didn't like being left behind in the pew on Sundays when we all filed up to the rail. The prospect of confession didn't faze him, he was honest and unafraid. He'd seen me enter the dark booth each Saturday morning and pop out unchanged. Confirmation was more mysterious. According to the nuns Confirmation would verify my faith, solidify my holiness, I'd be in the club for all eternity. Tenderfoot no more I'd shoot the Arrow of Light into full-blown Eagle Scouts for Christ. I'd see the way the truth the light. No more pledge, prospect, suspect. Confirmation was like joining a gang. Jesus would be tattooed actual-size on my body. Presumably we were the same height.

As for Phillip Madeira we hated him more now that to our intense chagrin he claimed hero status in the neighborhood, claimed Butch owed him for saving his life; claimed rock throwing wasn't always bad, thereby casting doubt on all our parental fears and directives. In confirmation class the nuns said I'd reached the age of maturity and reason. But I could not puzzle out the conundrum of Phillip Madeira. Confirmation would bestow upon me the holy spirit of right judgment and courage. I'd pick a new name. And not just any name but the name of a saint or biblical hero. Definitely not Cain or Judas. The Bishop would come to our church, smear oil on my head, shout out my new identity and expect a response from me at Mass in front of the entire congregation to confirm this boy wasn't just some idiot whiffleball player, some feeble example of an older brother, this boy would be a soldier of Christ. Yet the very existence of God seemed suspect, tainted with doubt, when faced with the reality of Phillip Madeira.

If our faith in God was strained by the tomato/rock/tumor incident, it was restored the day Madeira went to Fenway Park to see the Red Sox. Everyone's dad took them to Fenway at some point, but when Phil announced they had tickets we heard about it for weeks. Phil went everywhere wearing his glove and bragging about how he'd catch a foul ball or even a homer at Fenway. He named our most revered idols: Carl Yastrzemski, Rico Petrocelli, Tony Conigliaro—they'd hit the ball and Phil would catch it.

Baseball was huge in our neighborhood. I was an average all-around player. Butch was MVP four consecutive years in Little League. Phil was a total buffoon. He was top heavy with his fat head and his brogan-clad feet. He ran like a girl and couldn't catch a gently tossed beach ball. We did our best to ignore his bigheaded boasting, a test we figured, a chance to earn brownie points in heaven, but we were young boys, and we loved baseball and the Red Sox and trips to Fenway and we hated Phillip Madeira.

Finally, game day came and Mr. Madeira drove off with Phil and his older brother. We got up a whiffleball game and put the irritation behind us. It was October with the smell of fall in the air and we smacked and dove for the unpredictable plastic ball dipping and diving chaotically in the fading light. The days were not long and it was dusk when we saw the Madeiras' station wagon come back down the street. That wasn't right. Fenway Park was 30 minutes away and the game was a late game. They should not have been back this early. Butch and I charged up to Madeira's house and saw Phil hauled out of the car by his dad and brother, one on each side. "Keep your head back," they said to him. "Breathe through your nose."

Phil dragged his feet like a dead person, stared at the sky, and made wet moaning sounds. His open mouth was full of blood and broken-off teeth. There was blood all over his Red Sox shirt. We knew what had happened even before his brother blurted it out. "He got hit in the mouth with a ball."

"Ahaaaaa," Phil said.

"Where's the ball?" I said.

The dad gave me an evil Protestant Minister look. "You boys go home."

They dragged Phil into the house. Butch and I looked at each other in wonder. There is a God! We could have chalked the incident up to bad luck but the brother told us that it happened in the first inning. They'd settled into their seats, hadn't even ordered the peanuts and Crackerjacks. Phil was jumping around, smacking his glove, and mouthing off to anyone within earshot about catching a foul when there was a sharp crack and—Holy shit, here comes one! Everyone stood. Arms in the air. The brother said a big guy behind them had a clean shot at the ball but passed it up, telling Phil: "You got it kid, it's all yours, catch it!" And Phil standing there wide-eyed with his glove up over his head and his big fat mouth open, showing all his gappy teeth—Whap! The ball never even grazed his glove. Phil's mouth was plugged with the very thing that opened it. We didn't know the word irony but we still appreciated it.

If our faith in God was restored by the heavenly foul ball, it was an untested faith until the camping incident put it to the fire.

In Cub Scouts we prized our canteens, jackknives, folding entrenchment tools. But a tent was huge. A tent was the foundation of real camping, surviving in the wild, living off the land, or at least sleeping out in the backyard. Madeira was first to get a tent. His Dad brought it home from Sears one day in the spring and we grudgingly suspended our enmity for Phil so we could get some tent know-how, maybe even an invitation to sleep out in the elements.

None of us knew how to set up a tent. There were poles and stakes and tie-down cords and no adults to help us. Phil was feverish with excitement and conceit. We knew to stretch the canvas and pound the stakes into the ground through the corner rope loops. Phil was on one side pulling and pounding his stakes, Butch and me on the other. I pulled my corner to stake it down just as Phil pulled on his side. Butch stood there watching. Doing nothing. I was his older brother; he left it to me. No one noticed when I yanked my rope loop too hard and the cheap thing came off in my hand. Instinctively I dropped it and moved to the next corner. "Butch," I said quickly, to not distract Phil, "you do that corner." I nudged him toward the destroyed loop.

Butch innocently went to the corner I'd wrecked, picked up the torn-off loop and said: "What's this?"

Sadly, there is no way to put a positive spin on sending my brother like a lamb to be slaughtered. I knew Phil's reaction would be explosive and violent. I was afraid of Phil. I'd never have had the nerve to broad-jump onto his back.

"You broke it!" he screamed and pounced on Butch squatting awkwardly with the rope loop in his hands. Phil knocked Butch back onto the grass, pinned his shoulders to the ground and brought his cannonball head down on Butch's face. Repeatedly the head rose and fell like a hammer while I stood there, doing nothing.

The nuns said God doesn't distinguish between sins of passivity and deliberate acts. My sin was both, an act of cowardice and deceit. It was not hard to fear God's wrath watching my younger brother's face pounded into the dirt by Mad Madeira's head from hell.

When the beating was over, Madeira exhausted and my brother inert on the ground, Phil ran wailing to his mother. He would tell. Butch would get in trouble. My little brother rose without a sound, without my help, and started home, his back to me. I ran to catch up. Only when he turned to look at me did he begin to cry. His disappointed face, dirt-streaked and bruised, blood oozing from his nose, reflected the bright white clarity of God's illumination knob cranked up all the way.

We always walked to confession together on Saturday morning, Mom insisted on it, so Butch will be in the habit, she said. "You're his older brother, you set an example." I'd enter the confessional while Butch sat outside on the church steps. I'd run through the rigmarole with O'Gara, fake-pray my penance, and we'd be home corralling whiffle balls in an hour. But this sin I didn't know how to dispose of, how to admit, how to avoid. It was the first sin I remember being plagued by, my original sin. I told Father O'Gara I'd fought with my brother. I hurt him, bloodied his nose. I often lied in confession. An ironic compounding of wrongdoing and subsequent damnation that was not exactly lost on me as much as mired in confusion. I didn't know how to face truth, or recognize it, or ingest it. O'Gara gave me his standard penance: three Hail Marys and an Our Father. He didn't even ask me if I apologized.

I went up to the rail in front of the altar, knelt and prayed. For real. After three Hail Marys and an Our Father I said an Act of Contrition. I said one, then another. I didn't know what the word contrition meant, but I couldn't move, it was as if my body was wedded to the prayer rail. I knelt there while Butch waited outside, wondering where I was. After a while the heavy church door creaked open and banged shut and Butch crept down the side aisle under the stained-glass windows. His shadow fell on the marble floor next to me. He lingered, unsure what to do, seeing his older brother on his knees with bowed head and clasped hands.

I wanted him to go home, to know I set no example, that I was no soldier. I was a Weebelo Christian, weak in holy knot tying, deficient in godly merit badges, I had hit no home runs for goodness, caught no illusive balls. I knew then I'd take my brother's name, Joshua, for Confirmation. The Bishop would recite it loud for the entire congregation. Upon me the holy spirit of maturity, right judgment, and courage would descend. I'll know and be known. I'll be brave, set example for my young brother, I won't let him take a head thrashing for my weakness and fear. I'll leap fearlessly onto the backs of dragons and Protestants. Before me fat heads will fall.

But right then I couldn't move to tell him what to do. I turned and mouthed the words: Go Home. He shook his head and shuffled back down aisle. I heard the pew creaking where he sat in the back row, waiting all Saturday afternoon, while I knelt there reciting Acts of Contrition over and over, 50 maybe 100 of them. More prayers than I'd ever said in my life. They were nowhere near enough.

Nun Blood

I was related to one and had eight at school, plus Mother Gonzaga. They had black habits and black hearts and stiff white collars and bibs and wooden rosary beads like dull eyeballs around their waists. They swished down corridors like demented penguins, course habits swinging, precious beads rattling. Naturally I was fearful about having a nun for a relative. I certainly never told anyone at Saint Joe's that a nun, for Christ's sake, was related to me. I didn't even know nuns had relatives. In 1st grade I thought nuns were grown in convents, or maybe covenants, maybe like mold—the right conditions in a damp place, kind of dumb, like a dungeon where things develop in the dark. Or maybe priests had something to do with it. I didn't know but I certainly never expected nuns to have moms and dads and sisters and brothers. Here's my aunt the nun. Who would want to say such a thing? But apparently that's what she was, this spawn of my grandmother's sister, my mom's aunt, making her some kind of secondhand aunt to me. Her name is lost, I'm thinking Sister Bertrille, but that was the flying nun on TV. This was in the sixties. Whatever her name was, (maybe Agnes or Mary), we visited her at a convent not far from

Saint Joe's School. I was petrified one of my friends would see me and find out I had nun blood. We strolled the convent grounds, ate in the cafeteria, and did some phony praying in the chapel. And that led to goodbye hugging by my mom and grandmother. Then it was my turn. At Saint Joe's touching a nun was akin to lying naked in a poison ivy patch. I can still feel her heavy black habit, the body heat, the alien embrace that left me feeling engulfed, different. Not holy or saved or any crap like that. I don't know what I felt. I was in 2nd grade then with Sister Frankenstein, so called because she was tall and limped. Someone said she had a wooden leg.

In 3rd grade Sister Mary Magdalene claimed to have been present when Christ rose from the dead and we didn't doubt her. She looked like a crocodile standing upright in a nun's habit, long leathery face hanging toward the floor, pointed teeth in a wicked grin. She said the Civil War cards we collected were distributed by The Communists. She said Sonny & Cher were The Devil. She said bangs on boys grew into your forehead and infected your brain. "That's what wrong with those Beatles," she said. "They're insane because hair has grown into their brains."

Bucky Beaver in 5th had teeth like yellow woodchips that stuck straight out of her mouth. The Lip in 6th was a short troll-like creature with a major harelip.

The most serious nun afflictions could only be guessed at. The Lip liked to go into the boy's room to monitor our peeing. In catholic school you pee at a certain time. Before recess we'd file in—we were required to file everywhere—and stand at the urinals against the wall with the Lip walking up and down behind. Being anxious to get to recess we were inclined to pee and run. Lip said she was there for hygienic purposes. "Shake it off boys, shake it off and wash your hands. Nobody wants to see your pee-stained pants." We weren't sure what she wanted to see. If anyone went into a stall she'd look under the door. "What's your business in there? Hurry up."

The nuns ruined recess with rules. "Have fun," they commanded. "Don't stand against the fence. Run around. Not fast. No roughhousing. Line up—single file—walk!"

Boys and girls were separated. The classroom, cafeteria, the corridors were segregated: boys on one side, girls on the other. The playground had a white line down the middle. Sentry nuns stood at each end. If we stepped a foot over that line onto the girls side we were sent to the office which meant facing Mother Gonzaga, which I am sure prepared us for facing The Devil himself. There was nothing like detention, or writing something 500 Times on the board. All punishment was physical. Gonzaga had a long pointed stick with which she whipped our backsides. Pain was precursor to learning with these nuns. In class they used 16-inch rulers with steel edges to reprimand bad penmanship, low test scores, talking in class, passing notes. We did all those things.

"You! Daydreamer!" That was me. "Get up here!"

"Yes, Sister."

I stood at the front of the room, presented my palm open flat like an exposed griddle: WHAP! "God loves you." WHAP! "And so do I." WHAP! "That's why I want you to do well." WHAP! "Now sit down."

Because we learned from the nuns, because they taught us well, we were always on watch for ways to ridicule them. It was difficult because they were so devious. About the only one who seemed vulnerable was Bucky Beaver in 5th. She was soft spoken and didn't hit us or send us to Gonzaga. Bucky was probably likeable but she looked exactly like a Beaver, buck teeth and puffy cheeks as if full of crunched up nuts. We tortured her by drawing Beavers on the board, bringing stuffed Beavers to class. I found a cartoon Beaver named Bucky appearing in a toothpaste ad in Life magazine. I tore him out and stuck his picture up on the door of her classroom. To all of this she never reacted or said anything. She had long dark eyelashes that sometimes looked wet.

Because she was shaped like a Beaver and walked like one Bucky had trouble with her habit which was made for a human being not a large rodent. Bucky was always tripping over the hem of her habit or catching it on a chair leg or knocking her hip against our desks. When she taught she perspired heavily and then her headpiece would slide back leaving a barely visible dark hairline above her shiny forehead. Hair on nuns was strictly forbidden. They exposed no body parts except hands and face. I didn't even know nuns had hair until I saw Bucky. She was always pressing her headpiece forward and patting it down and I became more and more interested in seeing her hair. Anything marking a nun as a human being seemed curious. Sometimes a quarter inch of Bucky's hair was exposed, other times half an inch. "I'd like to see her lose that whole headdress," I said to my friend Bill Hogan one day at recess. We were passing time waiting for fat Allen Black to show up so we could slam him against the fence.

Hogan was one of the bigger kids in school and liked to bully people. He still greased his hair fifties style, though he combed it straight forward after the Beatles. "I'd like to see her lose the whole habit," he said.

"That might be scary," I said.

"What do you think a nun looks like naked?"

"I don't think nuns get naked," I said. "But the head thing, you know how it slips back? How she's always pulling it forward?"

"Yeah."

"Seems like it wouldn't take much to—"

"Hey Black!"

Hogan spotted Allen Black.

"Get over here Black!"

Poor Allen, fattest kid in town. Anyone paid him attention, even negative, he cooperated. "Hi," he said. He knew we would slam him against the fence. Hogan grabbed one wrist and I the other. We'd been slamming kids against the fence for years. The fence was a smooth wooden stockade, well over our heads. Allen was the best for this because he was so heavy. We stood him about two feet out with his back to the fence. Allen's back was like an overstuffed chair, huge and rounded. The fence was flat and somewhat forgiving. We wound up Black…one…kids watched and picked up the countdown…two…we swung him out by the wrists and whipped him back toward the fence, not letting him hit, just getting the momentum going. Kids were chanting: Allen Black, break his back. Allen was smiling and going along with it, moving his 300 pounds into the swing…three. We slammed his fat back into the fence as hard as we could. There was a tremendous Whump and the entire quarter mile of fence all the way down the playground to the garage rippled and rocked as if hit by a hurricane wind. Someday, if Allen's back held out, the fence would topple. The sentry nuns came running. We moved off, hands in our pockets.

"Look at her running," I said, pointing.

"Who?" Hogan said.

"Bucky," I said. "See how she holds her hand on her head. I'm telling you that head thing can come off."

"Yeah, why don't you go over there and pull it—see what happens."

"I bet I can get Lorenzo to do it."

Hogan looked at me and smiled. Jimmy Lorenzo would do anything. We found him in the garage next to the playground. It was an empty two car garage—strictly off limits. Nothing but years of built up oil stains and coagulated grime on the floor. We hid our cigarettes and matches behind a loose wallboard.

Lorenzo was smoking one after another. "Gimme a butt," Hogan said.

"Me too," I said.

"You fucking guys get your own butts," Lorenzo said. We stood with our hands out. Luckies. I took his lit one and sucked fire into mine.

"Man, you missed it," I said. "Bucky's headpiece slipped halfway off while she ran across the yard."

"Shit," he said.

"Hogan thinks we can get it to fall off in class," I said.
"How?"
"You got any fishhooks?"
"My dad does."
"See if you can get one, and about three feet of fishing line." Then the bell rang and we hid the butts and ran.

We slouched in late, stinking of smoke with our shirttails untucked and our hair down on our foreheads. We saw Mother Gonzaga in the corridor, small, wiry and black, pointing her knotty finger at us: "You three, halt. What is the meaning of this?" That was Gonzaga's favorite question because she knew we didn't know the meaning of anything.

"What?" I said.

"What!" She latched onto my hair. Her hands were razor wires. Her fingers had nails specially designed, maybe mutating over time, to inflict pain on small boys. It didn't matter how I answered her question, she always twisted a hank of my hair between her index finger and thumb and I buckled. "Stand up straight!" She attacked our genetic traits. "Why is your hair a mess?" I had thick curly locks that were easy to get a grip on. "President Kennedy parted his hair on the right. Why have you no part?"

"I don't know, Mother."

"You don't know!" She jerked my head in four directions, accentuating her syllables and punctuating her sentences with jolts to the head. "Haven't I told you…?" Push, pull, jerk, yank. "How many Times do I have to say…?" Tug, wrench, snatch, thrust. When I was dizzy and off balance she went for the face. Her dry scaly palms clapping hard with my face wedged between, her long fingers reddening my cheeks and ears together. When my face burned and my head felt like the clapper inside a bell, she grabbed my ear, spun me around and said: "Go to the end of the line I'll get you again."

Then it was Hogan's turn. He was tall and it was tough to grip his greasy hair but his ears tended to stick out and she snatched one and twisted him down to her level.

"Is this the way we come in from recess?"

"No Mother."

"No! I'll box your ears." She balled her claws into fists and pounded both of his ears at once, then spun him around. "End of the line, I'll get you again."

"James Lorenzo!" She grabbed a fistful of Jimmy's blonde hair. "Why do I smell smoke?"

"I don't know Mother."

"You don't know!" Pull, tug, yank, jerk.

Lorenzo was prone to painful ejaculation: "Whoa, Ugh, No, Ahaa." Which seemed to spur Gonzaga on.

"Why are you so short?"

"God made me this way?"

"God made you so you could smoke cigarettes and stunt your growth?"

"No Mother. Ahaa…"

I think she hated Lorenzo more than the rest of us because he was small and cute. He was caving in from the hair pulling, buckling and ignoring her order to "stand up straight." She let go of his hair and he dropped to his hands and knees in the middle of the corridor and bingo she nailed him in the butt with one of her killer nun shoes. Black leather, stub-nose toe as stiff as a shotgun barrel. "End of the line I'll get you again."

And she did. We went through painful shifts of this until she tired and said: "Get out of my sight, the lot of you."

We got to class red faces stinging and Lorenzo sat on one butt cheek for the rest of the day. I made the whole Bucky headdress thing seem like it was his idea. It didn't work right away because the fish hook Lorenzo brought in was too big. I had to go down to Grants Sporting Goods and swipe a tiny trout hook the size of a fingernail.

The nuns had heavy wooden chairs behind their desks. Some of them never sat but Bucky used her chair. In the late afternoons she sat reading her Catechism while we did our work. The bonnet or whatever it was, a shroud covering the head, shoulders, and breasts, came to a point in the back like a medieval hood, which hung over the back of the chair. One day during lunch I snuck into the room and looped the fishing line around the leg of her chair and dropped the fishhook beneath. The hard part was talking Lorenzo into going up there and hooking the hook into the tail end of Bucky's headdress. "Why me?" he wanted to know.

"It was your idea," I said. He knew he hadn't thought of it but didn't want to say that because he admired the idea and Hogan was standing there.

"You're the smallest," Hogan said. "She won't see you."

"What if she does?"

"She won't," I said. "You know Bucky. She doesn't see shit."

Lorenzo was sensitive about being short so a mission where smallness was an asset appealed to him. Because he was short he liked to do big things. He agreed to try the plan if Bucky let him clap the erasers. Hogan told all the usual eraser clappers to back off that day and about 2:45—eraser clapping time—Lorenzo got up and approached Bucky at her desk. She'd been up that afternoon, even pushed the chair in and out but never saw the tiny fishhook on the floor beneath her chair. Lorenzo put on his innocent face and said: "Excuse me Sister. May I please clap the erasers?"

Bucky nodded. "You may."

Eraser clapping was a privilege because you got to go unsupervised into the playground to smack the erasers against the wall. After that you had to clean the board and chalk shelf which was directly behind Bucky's chair. Lorenzo was a sneaky bastard. He dragged the special board-cleaning eraser in long slow strips until everyone quit watching him. He even dropped the eraser once and bent down behind Bucky's chair to eyeball the fishhook. It was right at his feet. When Bucky looked up at the clock and told us to put away our work and get ready to go there was paper rustling and book closing and chair shifting and for a second I thought it was too late, that Bucky was going to get up. But then while we all snapped our three-ring binders and shoved stuff into our desks I saw Lorenzo go down behind Bucky's chair. She completely obscured him so I never actually saw him bury the fishhook into the cloth habit. He was on his feet the instant she turned to look for him. "Are you still doing that?" She said. "Finish up, please."

"Yes, Sister."

We knew when it would happen. At 3:05 Gonzaga came on the intercom for final announcements. Bucky rose then and stood by the door. At 3:15 we went home. When I heard the beep of the intercom my heart raced. I kept my head down. I watched through my eyelashes. Bucky started to rise and was jerked back slightly just as Gonzaga said Excuse me Sisters and Students Please. Bucky pulled, but the fishing line was strong and the hook held in the fabric and the chair scraped against the floor and with us all watching the head covering slid off backward and Bucky let out a howl like a scalded cat. There was a second of shocked silence, then everyone was laughing and pointing. Through the intercom Gonzaga yelled Attention! Attention! Bucky's headdress was apparently attached to the habit somehow and Bucky twisted her torso and snatched at it with her arms where it hung across her back but couldn't manage to pull it up onto her head. If she had simply cried then we wouldn't have laughed. But she panicked and yanked at the headdress and finally ran from the room with one hand on her head and the chair following her to the door where it got stuck and the headdress ripped free and Bucky bolted down the corridor with it streaming behind her. The class jumped up and charged the door. Gonzaga shouted through the intercom. Hogan had the presence of mind to lift the chair, remove the fishhook and drop it into the wastepaper basket. The Lip heard the ruckus from across the hall in 6th and came out shouting at us to line up for the buses. The timing was perfect because when Gonzaga got there the buses were pulling in and she couldn't hold them up—we went home.

There were thirty kids in class and by some miracle,

Bucky's bulk, and Lorenzo's small stature, no one apt to say anything saw anything. I wasn't concerned about Hogan, the nuns taught us to lie well—keep the story short and stick to it. I worried Lorenzo might crack under Gonzaga's violent inquisition that went on for days but he never did. We had a good laugh at Bucky's expense and for all practical purposes got away with it.

Sort of.

The problem was Bucky herself. When the headpiece slipped back I don't know what I expected to see but it certainly was not the mass of long shiny dark hair that exploded from under the tight bonnet. No wonder she had trouble keeping the thing on her head, she had more hair than Joanne Dubuque, the most beautiful girl in school who had long golden banana curls down to her waist. Bucky was a young woman.

She never said a word about the incident. The next day she walked into the room wearing her headgear as if nothing had happened. But it had happened. And from the moment I saw her hair it was almost like touching a nun, or being related to one. I didn't think of her as Bucky anymore. Her name, was Sister Dolorous. I could not stop seeing her with the long silky locks bouncing behind her as she ran from the room, or picturing her face as it would be caressed and complemented by the hair if it were allowed to hang free. What's worse was the way she treated us, with even more kindness and care than before. As if she felt sorry for us. She was more reserved, as if she was disappointed, or couldn't be bothered with people like us. I found myself seeking her approval, trying harder on my lessons, even attempting to gain her affections. But she never conceded that I existed, and I left the 5th grade with a great sorrow that I could not give it another go.

Skin Tight

Dad drove. I was out cold in the passenger seat. He must have carried me to the car and buckled me in. Possibly some panic there, some sense of things gone wacko when your kid won't wake up on an otherwise typical weekday morning— as heavy as the dead when he tried to raise me for school. Not Again! I saw what he went through when Mom died six months ago. Now me too Dad must have thought, his son, the same feeling of helplessness and panic. Maybe it wasn't as bad, I had a pulse, a heartbeat, I was breathing. I surfaced briefly on the way to the hospital, my head rubbernecking on my shoulders, chin on chest, drooling mouth. I saw Dad way over on the other side of the car, about a mile away, the space between us watery as if I was looking through old Coke bottles. Dad's mouth was moving but I couldn't hear anything. He was dressed for the office. I felt like giggling. What am I doing in the car in my pajamas? It was a school day, 7th grade, 1967.

Each night before bed, I checked to see what I'd wear the next day. I'd spent the previous seven years buttoned down with nuns in a parochial school. Starched white shirts, maroon neckties, sensible trousers, a sharp blazer. The public school's free form dress policy was a blessing like the nuns never offered. Without a mom to oversee my wardrobe, I wore what I wanted. I created a new version of myself, a hip 1967 image religiously upheld.

The night before this morning my closet was compromised. My flowered shirts and wide belts were there but no pants, at least no pants I'd be seen in. Mod-era pants were tight and short—think James Brown. This was before the raggedly patched-up blue jean look that finished off the sixties. Bellbottoms were a year away. The point is, I had nothing to wear. My two pairs of prized black pants, so tight I had to lie down on the bed to pull them on, which I wore with a pair of pointy-toed "Beatle Boots," were in the wash. I must not have staggered them into the laundry basket. I was usually careful because we had to care for ourselves now. I couldn't yell, "MOM! Where's my black pants?" and have June Cleaver appear saying, "Why here they are honey, I was just pressing them for you."

Nothing like that could happen in this house because there was no June Cleaver, there was no Mom anymore. There was only Mrs. Bent, a woman Dad hired to clean and do laundry, not that we could afford a maid, or afford to be picky about pants. Dad was an accountant who wore Father Knows Best suits with wingtips and a fedora. He would not be sympathetic to my plight. If I started griping about tight black pants, I could end up forcibly delivered to school in a pair of baggy beige corduroys with cuffs. Cuffs! "Perfectly good pants young man—you'll wear them." Them is what was hanging in my closet—always hanging in my closet because I never wore them and I never would wear them. I'd rather die than be seen in baggy beige corduroys with cuffs.

Or sick maybe. Really sick. Sicker than I could fake. I'd faked sick too often and Dad wouldn't fall for it. He recently caught me putting the thermometer on the radiator—stupid thing popped its top and spit tiny mercury balls all over the floor. Dad thought I bit down on it. Did you cut your mouth? Let me see! He had anxious mornings because it was solely him trying to get four boys up, fed, dressed and off to school while preparing himself for a day at the office. I'd fake sick, my brothers wouldn't get up, no one would eat breakfast. Dad farted up and down the stairs in a white shirt and shaving lotion shouting Damn you boys! Damn these mornings! What relief he must have felt arriving at work in his suit, hat and briefcase in hand, huge wingtips squeaking on the polished floor, passing orderly rows of desks in the secretary pool, nodding to the admiring glances—they knew he was a widower now—the cubicles lined up true, his adding machine, slide rule, ledger books full of numbers that only added up one way. Work must have been a refuge from the pain and chaos at home. But that wasn't something I considered. I considered myself. I considered the need to convince Dad I was legitimately sick so I could lie in bed all day while my black pants were laundered and returned to my closet. The question was how to look truly sick.

The answer was medicine. Pills, capsules, tablets, vials of them in our downstairs bedroom. Mom was in and out of the hospital but she died at home. She was quiet then, too weak to climb stairs. She was always in bed, next to which, on the night table, and more on the bureau: Drugs. Reds, blues, greens, half yellow-half speckled, and shiny little blacks, plus some potent smelling syrups and pastilles. I wasn't drug smart. I didn't know Vicodin from Vapo Rub. They didn't even have Vicodin then. Whatever they did have I figured a few pills down the hatch might induce some puking, some pasty pallor or feverish tackiness might be raised by ingesting a haphazard concoction. I'd look flushed, pale, even peaked. Pea-kid. A word Mom used. I had no idea what it meant. All I knew was if I nodded yes to it and hung my head like I was dying, she used to let me stay home from school. So that was my goal: pale, peaked, and puking.

I overshot the goal a bit. I wasn't a doctor. I saw baggy corduroys in my closet, my social life on the line, salvation in preparations. I'd rig the morning wakeup call, the pills a way out—not all the way out, I wasn't trying suicide, although I came close. I fiddled with the vials: popped a few greens, hopped a couple reds, the remedy in the combinations. A random handful, an arbitrary headfull. I downed them helter-skelter and went to bed and was soon well beyond dreams, beyond expectations, well into a well, a pit, a hole, down and down and down and well-well-well— What's this? Waking up in the car in my PJs? Coke bottles affixed to my eyeballs? I'd never taken drugs, not even beer or wine, pot was a year or two off. The sensation wasn't unpleasant. That was the strange thing, I never did get sick, I was whacked out, half dead even—I never knew how close I came to not coming back—but I was not sick. I recall the car, Dad driving, his mouth moving, then nothing until someone stuck a knife in my back—one of those bone-handled Jim Bowie jobs that pioneers threw into trees. That's how it felt anyway, extreme pain in a white and chrome room, gone was the coke-bottle effect, more like starbursts and lightning bolts, amazing how a knife in the back promotes acuity, everything vivid and true. Nurses and orderlies said "Don't move." Of course I moved. Someone was Roto Rootering my spine with a spear. I squirmed like a stuck slug. At hospitals they tell you what to do without saying why, "Don't move, it will hurt." It hurt already and I wanted to know what "it" was. But I couldn't talk. I was pinned down on my side while they applied acute abuse to my lower back while all went black.

I surfaced again sitting up with wires attached to my head. The electric chair! Red, green, blue—a wire for every pill—the wires hooked to a machine, a white-coat guy studied my face and twisted knobs with glee. Gauged needles flickered, machines whirled and moaned, something was burning. Give me my bedroom in the well of vacuity without proper pants, give me my closet, give me beige corduroys with cuffs, I'll wear the pants I would have told them if they had communicated with me instead of stabbing my vital parts with knives and electric wires. I didn't want to die. I just wanted to get sick enough to not have to go to school looking like a chump. So I'm an idiot. So I'm dangerously dumb. But I was cool at school by God. There were no baggy-ass corduroys on this guy's ass.

At some point I knew I would live if they didn't kill me trying to figure out what was wrong. I could have saved everyone time, money, and trouble, but they didn't ask, and I couldn't talk, and they continued to test, and I surfaced and sunk and finally woke in a regular hospital bed flat on my back unable to move with a big fat nurse standing over me, my head and lower back married to intense pain. The fat nurse said, "Well, Rip Van Winkle. How are we?"

"Headache," I said. "Back pain. I'm paralyzed."

"Spinal tap will do that," she said. "You weren't supposed to move."

I found sticky gauze patches and snippets of cloth-tape stuck to my head.

"Brain wave test," she said, "leaves a mess."

Spinal tap. Brain waves. Serious stuff. And painful. For three days I couldn't move because of the spinal tap gone wrong. My fault they said. "We told you not to move." The lower back pain wouldn't have been so bad but severe headaches were alleviated only by elevating my head, which I couldn't do because of the back. I couldn't sleep or eat and they wanted me to sit up, walk around even. I whined and cried until the fat nurse shoved her finger up my ass. That's how it felt anyway. I didn't understand the first few times what was happening. I wore standard uncool hospital garb split open up the back. She rolled me onto my side and applied firm rubber-glove pressure to my anus and instantly vibrant euphoric warmth swept through my body. I heard birds chirping, violins playing, I heard the word suppository and knew it wasn't her finger rushing me to anal bliss. She was shoving something up there and it was good. She wouldn't do it more than once a day. "You'll get hooked," she said.

The fat one was Day Shift, busy battle-ax RNs, white stockings with a seam up the back, the cocky folded cap pinned to their heads, a nun-like uniform in virginal white—effective and authoritative. They rousted me early for breakfast, changed my sheets like magicians. Said Yes Doctor to mumbling men in suits who shined lights in my eyes, listened to my heart, all the stereotypical stethoscope stuff.

The doctors had hairy knuckles and wore cufflinks and stayed about a minute.

"How do you feel?"

"Headache," I said, "backache."

"That's normal."

Interns and student docs in surgical scrubs and sneakers were about all day. They seemed to have nothing but time, reading my chart and engaging me in conversation as if we were pals, like big brothers, trying out their compassion to see if they actually had any, testing their theories about my case. "So," they'd say, rubbing their chins, "severe headaches, hmmm. Could be mental."

The fat nurse shooed them away. "Let's go Rip Van Winkle—Bath time."

"I'm in bed all day," I said, "how dirty can I be?"

Bath time sucked. The bathroom was cold and echoey with tile floor and stainless steel tubs and water way too hot and soap smelling like rat poison. "Strip," the fat one said. "Come on, come on. I've seen it all."

And there was always screaming from the burn kid.

He was five or six with sandy hair cut soup-bowl style, and he was all over the ward visiting those of us too lazy to get out of bed. He was precocious and personable this kid, the high spot of the ward. Most of his skin was missing. His body was burnt to raw meat and wrapped in gauze like The Mummy.

"How'd you get burned?" I asked him.

"Hot water on a jiggly chair."

Sometimes he was confined to his room because infection drove his fever up. But if he wasn't, he'd show up in my room after breakfast. "Hello," he'd say. "Would you like to play dominos?" We dumped the dominos out on the table. Inside the box were directions for Pip and Chickenfoot, but mostly the kid liked a game he made up called Train, which was more story than game. We connected the dominos where the dots matched up and invented the trips we would take if we weren't stuck in the hospital. Always places like Texas and China.

At bath time the nurses snuck in to get him and the screaming would start. He was horrified of baths. His burn dressing had to be changed daily and the only way to remove the gauze where it dried crusty to his oozing burns was to soak it off in hot water. The kid wanted nothing to do with hot water. He'd see them coming and the dominos flew. The fat one would trap him in a corner or under a bed and drag him screaming to the bathroom. His skin was gone from his lower chest down his stomach to his thighs and onto the tops of his feet. His penis was a pointed charcoal briquette. The tip had slipped off with the outer skin leaving a beet-colored stub. Listening to him scream in the steel bathroom was worse than the spinal tap. I was afraid the fat nurse would lose patience one day, forget her Florence Nightingale oath and hold him under to stifle his screams, letting the hot water fill his nose and mouth.

Afterward, wrapped in fresh gauze, his face red and swollen from crying, he looked hurt. He didn't know why they did it to him. "Infection" they said, but he didn't understand.

His parents came in the evenings, the mother chewing gum and the husband in a janitor uniform. They had an infant at home, these people, the mother, who'd left boiling water on a jiggly chair in the vicinity of a five-year-old, my friend, the domino kid.

My dad came too after work, his suit wrinkled from eight hours at the office and the rush-hour drive across town. He'd stay a while looking worried, drained, tired, then drive 40 minutes home to retrieve my brothers from the babysitter.

The rhythm of the ward was chaos early, then a long boring calm when the doctors and day nurses went home. I had a private room with a window looking out on the corridor. Student nurses showed up and stayed all night. Like the young interns, they were animated and happy to be fussing over us. Unlike the RNs in their institutional whites, the night nurses wore uniforms of pink and yellow or simply lab coats thrown over street clothes. They were girls. I was fifteen. One wore a red checkered outfit that snapped up the front. She had blonde bangs to her eyebrows and breasts like bob apples that pushed peeking gaps between the snaps. The hospital beds were high and at night a steel rail was raised on both sides. To raise it the bob-apple girl bent low over the bed, there was the hint of cleavage, and after the railing was up she'd fold her arms on top of it and rest her boobs atop her arms and talk to me as if she had all the time in the world. Sometimes a few night nurses would congregate in my room, surely hiding from their supervisor. I'd be King Shit then--Thank You God!--wondering how I'd gotten so lucky. One evening during visiting hours I was sitting up eating a cheeseburger and surrounded by a bevy of beautiful nurses when in walked my civics teacher Mr. Carolli. He eyeballed the nurses, looked at me munching the burger and said: "You don't look like you're hurting."

"Oh, I am," I said, "I'm in constant pain and agony."

He chuckled, "Yeah, I see that." At school he reported my circumstances to my cronies and I gained instant celebrity status. Among 7th-grade boys nothing was cooler than seductive nurses, skipping school, and cheeseburgers. I'd have stayed in the hospital for the rest of my life; anyone would—waited on hand and foot, attention at the touch of a call button, the touch of beautiful nurses. But the truth is, I was often hurting. At night the headaches were so bad I couldn't sleep. One night, as a last resort, I pressed the call button. I didn't want to, because I knew what I wanted, and I knew who would come, and she did, the bob-apple girl, her breasts rested on the bedrail.

"Problem?"

"My head," I said. I was in tears. "It hurts. Can't sleep."

She studied my chart. "Too soon," she said, "you just had something."

"The pills don't work."

"You have to wait," she said.

I couldn't say what I wanted, not to this nurse. "Please." I asked with agonizing looks. "Something that works, like the day nurse gives, the big one." I tried to indicate by mental telepathy, by teary-eyed longing, but the beautiful nurse looked perplexed.

"What?" She said. "What do you want?" Pointing was out of the question. She grew impatient. "I don't know what you want." I might have murmured the word behind. I must have said something. I didn't know any medical lingo. I was fifteen. A goddess stood before me. I needed her to shove something up my ass. Somehow, she got the idea. I think I annoyed her to the point where she was going to make me say it. She looked me straight in the eye, her breasts pressing the rail. "Suppository? Is that what you want?" Horrified. I couldn't I even nod. She shook her head and left. When she came back, I already was on my side, my face buried in the pillow. I never looked at her again. The incident made me want to leave the hospital and return to school.

They were done with me anyway. After a week they discharged me without understanding what happened. They never asked. I never said a word. At home I was allowed to move downstairs to the convalescent room. Dad decided it was time to use that room again. It was crowded upstairs with my brothers and I was the oldest. My first night home Dad was in the room clearing the night table and bureau of Mom's leftover pill vials—sweeping them with his hand into a trash bag. It had been six months but he hadn't previously had the time or courage to address this room. He glanced over at me sitting on the bed, paused, and said, as if the thought just occurred to him. "You never touched any of Mom's medicine?"

"Of course not," I said, as if that were the craziest notion in the world.

The next day was school. In the closet hung my two pairs of skintight black pants, freshly pressed, accomplices it seemed. That morning when I stretched out on the bed to pull on my pants, as I dragged them up my legs, I felt the little burn kid's skin sloughing off under the boiling water. I felt the dried-on gauze torn by the fat nurse while he was held down screaming in the bath. I saw his swollen red face, and the burnt-black stub of his penis. And me, with my baggy pants.

The Trestle

Crossing the trestle is trespassing. A black & white sign: DANGER KEEP OFF. We don't. We run the tracks, two Mikes, Debbie Martelli, and me, high stepping every other tie, avoiding the gaps, trying not to trip and tumble. A misplaced foot, a train coming on—we've seen the cartoons, the wedged foot, the wailed appeals. But we're kids, luck carries us.

The river is wide and the way around long—from the junior high school, through Barnsdale center, uphill past the cemetery and down County Road to the concrete bridge near the police station—and we're late. Out of detention at 3:30 with no ride, part of the punishment it seems, school and parents creating an insurmountable obstacle: You will stay after school one hour. You will not be home late. How is that supposed to work exactly? On foot it takes an hour to cover the 2.8 miles to our homes in Barnsdale Heights and that's only if we use the trestle and don't stop at the drugstore. We always stop at the drugstore. "I need cigarettes," Debbie says. She buys us coffee with her tip money—she works at her family's restaurant. Me and the two Mikes are always broke. Gossipy girls with blue eye makeup sit in booths sucking on straws. Seventh-grade punks at the magazine rack shove Playboy down their pants. Big Mike looks twenty-years-old in the ninth grade. He's got bruises and scars. "My old man," Mike says. "He's a bastard."

I'm closer to Crazy Mike, been to his house, met his smiley mother. She gives us snickerdoodles and Kool-Aid. She lets him drive her car because he has a learner's permit. He's in love with Debbie Martelli. Girls in our school are sticks. Short skirts and stuffed bras. Except Debbie. She's advanced—big tits. She's famous for what she supposedly does under the trestle bridge.

The two Mikes live on Ribbon Street and have been friends since kindergarten. Big Mike is a Neanderthal, receding forehead, prominent brow ridge, receding in general. He's stoic says our English teacher, Mrs. Macintyre, which we take to mean doesn't talk much. Macintyre says we're rude, crude, and socially unattractive. She also says she loves us. Especially Crazy Mike. He's Macintyre's pet. She worries over him, pushes his black hair off his forehead where the skin is stretched thin and a wishbone vein pulses. She calls him handsome but the blue-eye-makeup girls scoff and move away. Crazy Mike talks all the time. Verbose, Macintyre says.

One day, Crazy Mike and I are out in the middle of the trestle walking home from detention. Debbie is at work. Big Mike is beat up somewhere. The river is black and the wind cuts in from the ocean, seagulls fly and cry and crows walk and squawk and Crazy Mike says, "watch this" and drops to his stomach on the end of a cross tie and goes feet first over the edge. We're forty feet off the water whirlpooling around vertical timbers supporting the tracks. I'm thinking suicide—goodbye Crazy Mike.

Crazy Mike isn't called crazy based on whacky behavior. We're 15, half the school is crazy in that way, but something is genuinely wrong with him. His grin is a grimace, upper and lower teeth ground to stubs, black glossy pupils zone out his entire eyeballs. Fearful? Fearsome? No, fervor, that's the word Macintyre uses, feverous and zealous, that's Crazy Mike.

I lean over the edge and see the top of his head. The wind parts his hair showing his skull snow white as he shimmies down using fist-size nuts and bolts for handholds then crabs around to the backside of the timber and drops out of sight. "Chicken," he says, a voice from below. I have to do it because he did. Feet first over the edge, bear-hugging the timber. I slide down and come to the narrow space. Crossbeams abut to form a hidden spot beneath the tracks, an ancillary of construction maybe, a place to store rail spikes and baseplates. "A hidey hole," Mike says. Tight cozy quarters out of the wind, a crushed cardboard box to sit on.

This is the spot, says Crazy Mike, where they take Debbie to do whatever it is she does. But there is no "they". Crazy Mike is a notorious liar, he claims his father is famous in California. And it's well rumored at school that whatever Debbie does concealed within the trestle she does only with Big Mike.

When the four of us are together Crazy Mike isn't so

talkative, he keeps an eye on Big Mike. Crazy Mike looks up to Big Mike because of what he gets to do with Debbie Martelli. Envy and longing are our primary states. I've never been with a girl that way and I know Crazy Mike hasn't either and Big Mike isn't saying much, him being stoic and all, and his reticence makes Crazy Mike more paranoid and jumpy than he normally is. Big Mike's response to most things is curt and profane. "Motherfucker," he mumbles, "cocksucker." Profanity is uncouth, loutish, and socially unattractive, Mrs. Macintyre says.

Debbie too, keeps an eye on Big Mike, because she likes him, better than she likes us I guess, or in a different way. She walks close to him down the tracks through the woods to the trestle, a long straightaway from the center to the river. If a train is in sight we wait or run. Rattletrap trains moving slowly—freight, scrap metal, graffiti, no sleek people movers. We look forward and back, mark the train, Debbie says wait or go. We're all in love with her.

If we go with a train in sight the decision has to be spot-on because once out on the trestle there's no turning back. It's eyes down and hopping ties double time, stutter stepping rapid fire, no time to look around. We get over the river and stand aside the tracks on the gravel. The train lumbers by, engineer points at us and shouts. We give him the finger. We throw rocks. Crazy Mike gets frantic with rocks, firing them down on fishermen passing under the trestle.

The police station is right there by the County Road Bridge not a hundred yards from the trestle, a white stucco building with big unshaded windows overlooking the river.

Do those cops never look? Are they too lazy to get out of their donut chairs? The trestle is a quarter-mile long, the rail ties a foot apart. The span isn't sprintable—it takes time to hopscotch across. Are we invisible? A half-dozen officers, two or three detectives, all they have to do is look out the window, grab their suitcoats and keys, zip across the bridge to Barnsdale Heights Road to nab us coming off the tracks. Hey, you kids! A little fear of God, a trespassing citation, a phone call to our parents, might have saved pain and heartache later. But no.

We're left alone. No one sees us apparently. Every day we walk into the drugstore and steal stuff. We envy kids who live near the center of town. They call us the Barnsdale Heights gang. Big Mike counts for two or three people, Debbie is infamous and sought after, Crazy Mike is crazy. I'm the new guy, living until seventh grade in West Barnsdale where I went to St. Joe's and got walloped by nuns. In junior high, we get detention: three nights, five nights, we skip out and get more nights. It adds up, we lose track, we're always in detention. Big Mike is absent a lot. Cuts and bruises. No one cares. At my house coming home late draws parental ire. There are chores, reprimands, assignments. Sweeping the garage, weeding the garden, pushing a lawn mower. Things I'm not good at.

I'm good at shoplifting paperbacks: The Confessions of Nat Turner, The Eighth Day, The Bridge Over the River Kwai. "Try the library," Macintyre says. "You won't end up in jail." I steal Harold Robbins novels for the sex. Macintyre is amused. "At least you're reading."

Big Mike steals Zippo lighters and pipe tobacco. Tries

to appease his old man with these. Crazy Mike steals rubbers, shows them off as if he has a use for them. Debbie steals Slim Jims and O'Henry bars. "Bad for my skin," she says.

We're slick, unsightly, socially unattractive. We come and go, we're together, we're apart, we never know from day to day if we will ever see each other again. We assume we will but that's because we're teenagers steeped in self-importance and confusion. We expect things to go on as they always have which makes no sense because it is 1970 and nothing has been going on in any way consistent past or present. Our days are mazy, tortuous paths. We look for ways through. We hide in the spot within the trestle under the tracks. We cling to each other, smoke cigarettes and wait. Something will come, we know that much.

Trains are felt before heard. Mere sensation first, too slight to be called feeling, whatever comes before vibration. It starts with steel. An announcement from the rails above, then nuts and bolts galvanize and washers the size of dinner plates start humming. Timbers cut from whole trees angle up from the water and crossties black with creosote come to life, groan in resignation, shoulder the burden and sound off in a mounting uproar that grows until the daylight dims, the sky disappears. The train is above us and we're all screaming and deafened in the dark with the trestle creaking and shaking and the jangling nuts and bolts offering no assurance that trembling struts won't fall loose and the ties above crack and the rails twist and collapse and the train come down upon us. We roar because everything else does. Our eyes blur. Debbie grabs Big Mike's arm. Crazy Mike's teeth clench. This is as free as we ever get, trapped beneath the train, locked into a place from which we cannot move. There are no choices here. The engines alone weigh twenty tons. We can't look up. Dust and grit and slivers of something mist down upon our heads, a veneer, fallout. Everything merges. We're part of something—we have no idea what. There is no school, we have no parents, we are not late. We're primal—chaos our only comfort. If we disappear at this moment we imagine no one will notice.

When the train is gone we're buzzed and depleted, worked over, rushed out, down from a high. The trestle slows its breathing. We climb out, safe in silence. The world could be ended but for the wind. It's always windy on the trestle and it rains constantly. And now we're late.

Crazy Mike wears a wristwatch with a wide leather band. "Four-thirty," he says, when we hit Barnsdale Heights Road.

"My old man's going to beat my ass," Big Mike says.

"You want me to go in with you?" Debbie says.

"Motherfucker. Cocksucker."

"Tell him you were with me."

Big Mike's dad is Big Mike quadruple. Whatever came before Neanderthals. Outboard motors hang from trees in his front yard. Ribbon Street dead ends at the salt marsh where Crazy Mike has a Boston Whaler. We take it out, fish the cove, rake black mud for quahogs.

When the two Mikes head down Ribbon I walk on with Debbie. She lives in a new house overlooking the river. "Let's run," she says, for which I'm grateful. Walking alone with Debbie makes my bowels churn. "Race to the next telephone pole," she says.

It's uphill all the way. We run a pole, then walk a pole, winded. Run one, walk one, making our way along in phone-pole segments. I say stupid things. "Do you like field hockey?" She knows I'm a dork but it's okay. "How many nights you got?"

"No idea," she says. Detention is a self-perpetuating mystery. It's hard to recall the original infractions, how one thing leads to another. "I got five nights for skipping science," she says, "three more for skipping detention, then got caught smoking so…How many is that?"

Being the sole companion of a girl shuts down my brain, and Debbie isn't even a girl, she's a fully-formed woman. Most alluring in her waitress uniform. Checkered green and white with snaps gaping up the front. Everything Debbie wears is tight, not tight by design like the stuffed-bra girls in blue eye makeup, but tight like whale skin, her body pushes out. When she's not at the restaurant, she wears blue jeans and thick sweaters. Mohair or something, puffy.

"Run," she says at a pole, "now walk." I wait for clues, for words that don't sound as if they come from a lobotomized aardvark. If I pass Math and Science I'm headed for the high school—I should know how to talk to girls. Mrs. Macintyre says I'm going to college or jail. After we've run/walked about a hundred telephone poles there is a bond between Debbie and me. We're connected by phone poles, sweat, laugher, heavy breathing, and once in a while we bump shoulders. We're close in a way, not the way I'd like to be close to someone like Debbie, but something I don't have with anyone else. At the end of her driveway she says, "So long, see you tomorrow."

I love you, meet me under the trestle. "Bye," I say.

By Thanksgiving, rain is mostly sleet which means ice on the trestle. White ice crunches underfoot and crumbles, black ice is hard and slippery. Last winter Debbie fell and broke her wrist. Snow doesn't collect, too windy. There is frozen bird shit. Gulls cry overhead and crows squawk on the trestle ahead of us. "Sounds like they're quacking," Crazy Mike says. Nobody says anything. "I mean the sound they make. Doesn't it sound like quack-quack-quack…?"

Big Mike says, "Shut up."

December, January, we freeze. Detention is the same. We get out late, walk, footwear inadequate, it's dark by 4:30. In class Macintyre wears heavy plaid, like sofa material. She's huge and paces between our desks, a woman who loves us. "What would I do without you?"

She calls Crazy Mike "Michael J" since his middle name is James. She protects him on reading days. Up and down the rows, kid after kid, paragraph after paragraph, Macintyre calling out: "next"--"next"--"next"… All the books are the same. Heathcliff wants to fuck Cathy, Gatsby wants to fuck Daisy, Holden wants to fuck anyone. Crazy Mike always gets an easy paragraph. Macintyre keeps him off the hot seat, out of the griddle of snickers and smirks, blue-eye-makeup eyes rolling because he can't read worth shit and if he gets frustrated he stutters, the wishbone vein pumps, his face goes beet, he flies into a rage and look out the book sails across the room. We keep watch, ready to duck and dodge. Macintyre reads fast ahead spotting hard words coming up:

rural, crocodile, imbecile. When he's sweating and stuttering Macintyre pushes hair from his eyes, forehead vein pulsing about to p-p-p-pop. "Next," she says.

Crazy Mike is no good in Phys Ed either. He's got skinny legs and is ridiculed by Coach Larry Duchene, an asshole with a cleft palate who loves Big Mike. All the coaches love Big Mike, but—we're so grateful for this—Big Mike hates sports. He especially hates football. All his life fat men like his father have been coming up to him and saying, "I'll bet you play football!"

"Cocksuckers, motherfuckers."

Big Mike hates jocks and if he catches one alone, which is hard because they're herd animals, he flattens him on general principle, no question, cause, or reason. A jock walks out of the drug store, Mike bumps him up and says, "I don't like the way you look," then mashes his fist into the guy's face so hard he's out cold before his head hits the sidewalk. That's what Big Mike would like to do to Coach Duchene. He hates him because of what Duchene does to kids like Crazy Mike, the nerds, the ungainly, the inept at punt, pass, and kick.

We never want to go to Phys Ed and one day Crazy Mike has his mother's car. "Let's skip," he says. "Drive to Seekonk Speedway." It's getting close to the end now, high school across town in the fall if we pass, if we live that long. The car is a big Buick Riviera, 1967, sky blue. Debbie and Big Mike wed together in the backseat, mash down, make out. Filthy snow is sheared hard alongside the two-lane road heading inland away from the water, big black oaks and elms stand frozen, seatbelts are shoved beneath white leather bucket seats, slippery, vast carpeted floor, leg room from here to hell, and not a damn thing to hang onto, to brace against. Crazy Mike drives like Crazy Mike. I hang onto the door, the car fishtails through the curves, Mike laughs like a devil. I try to act cool, but he knows.

Welcome to Seekonk Speedway. We're welcomed with padlocked gates. Mike's dark eyes glaze over. Teeth grind. Forehead vein pulses. Debbie and Big Mike raise their heads, mash back down, the car heats up. Crazy Mike is unprepared for this disappointment. I wait for the explosion, the frenzied rage, the head pulsing to pop. He appears to be in a trance. His face is a mask. He moves the chrome shifter to reverse, backs away from the gate. Seekonk Speedway is closed. The day spreads out before us. Debbie is making mewing sounds from the backseat. The Riviera is 4500 pounds of steel powered by a 425 cubic inch engine. "Now, Mike," I say, "we can go to the beach." He's stone, staring, the jaw grinding. "How about Newport Creamery? You like the creamery." He's not hearing me. He pushes the pedal into the carpeting. The car surges forward and he snaps abruptly into crazed laughter. We're all dead. He's in control now, for once in his life he gets to say what will happen and there's nothing anyone can do about it. Crazy Mike senses fear emanating from my side, and, like a shark at a feeding frenzy, it spurs him on. He hangs the car way out on the curves, tires screech, a hubcap flies into the trees. I smile, ha, ha, wow, that was a close one. He knows I'm terrified and goes hard on the gas, roaring into the turns, increasing the margin for error. After a particularly close call he turns his head from the road—we're going 90 mph—he looks closely at my face, makes sure I'm petrified. He twists his head to the backseat and jerks the wheel hard, as if to knock Debbie and Mike out of the car. His crazed crooked grin is pure ecstasy. It's the happiest I've ever seen him. The day of our death.

But no. We don't die, not yet anyway. We get detention for skipping. Mike's mom takes the car away. We huff and puff in the despairing days of February. We hit the drugstore, sip coffee, and steal shit. We trudge the tracks to the trestle. There are ice floes in the river. The police station windows are fogged with cop breath. We're frozen and want to zip across but a train appears. It's Valentine's Day, by chance, and we've stolen red heart boxes of chocolates from the drug store. "Wait," Debbie says, hugging her hearts.

"We can make it," Crazy Mike says.

"No way," she says, "too close."

Crazy Mike quakes head to toe, shivers from impatience, from the cold, from the ache of desire. Debbie rubs cherry lip balm on her mouth, wipes her nose, puffy breath. We're ankle deep in snow. Big Mike takes off a glove, snaps open his Zippo, lights a cigarette in the wind. "Debbie's right," he says. "We should wait."

Crazy Mike says, "No, no, come on, I'm freezing." He wants us to listen to him.

"Forget it, Mike," Debbie says. "It's coming too fast."

"We can make it!"

Big Mike sucks hard on the butt, looks back at the train, looks at me. "Chuck, what do you think?"

"I don't know," I say.

We know stalling isn't good, if we're going to go we need to go. But Debbie's firm. "No, Mike. Don't do it."

He does it. Takes off, hitting every third tie, slipping on black ice, crunching on white. "He's gonna bust his ass," Big Mike says.

We look at the train, look to Crazy Mike. "Idiot," Debbie says. "Why does he have to do things like this?"

For you, he does them for you. "He'll make it," I say. I'm pretty sure he will, the trains move slow across the trestle, predictable, nothing new ever happens, except when it does. Come what may, Macintyre always says, May will come.

The train comes at us, a black speck growing larger, gradually filling the white sky. Up ahead on the trestle, Crazy Mike scrambles. There is no room to stand aside and let it pass. "He won't make it," Debbie says.

"He has to make it," I say.

Big Mike spits, tosses his cigarette butt. "He's gonna be a grease stain."

Debbie jumps onto the tracks waving her arms at the train. I follow her lead, we holler and shout but the engineer has his window shut tight, glazed over with ice. The last we see of Crazy Mike, he's paused in the middle of the trestle. Debbie screams, "Don't stop!" He's looking back at us and grinning his crazy grin. He wants to be sure we see him out there, balls to the wall, pedal to the metal, bolder than brass. He raises his arm to wave, then the train rumbles by blocking him out.

"He's a goner," Big Mike says.

But there is the spot, the hidey hole, and Crazy Mike knows exactly where it is. We run towards the trestle and see him at the last moment slide over the edge, shimmy down the timber.

"He's got it," Debbie says.

But it's so rock-hard cold, all the days of snow and sleet, maybe the timbers are slick, handholds iced over, or so raw to the touch Mike's fingertips can't hang on. He's clinging, we see that clearly, about to crab around to our hidden spot of safety under the tracks, then just as clearly and seemingly with no time passing, he's off the beam in midair forty feet over the water.

"Holy shit," Big Mike says.

The train rolls. We don't hear his body hit the water. It's instant fast and Debbie is screaming and hauling ass, hearts in hands, for the police station while me and Big Mike clamber down the frozen weeds and black rocks to the water's edge. Crunchy white ice skirts the shore, and under the trestle where the water pools up around the timbers there are floes of clear black ice the size of car hoods. Through one of these we see Mike's white face pressed up from the dark below with his mouth wide open as if to fog a window.

"He's dead," Big Mike says. He looks at me, looks at the police station. "We're gonna be fucked."

I look to Big Mike. I'm the new guy here, the two Mikes have always been together. That's his best friend under the ice. We run back up the rise, across the tracks, hide in the trees and watch the cops come from the station in flapping suitcoats led by Debbie. They're on their radios, Debbie is pointing to where Mike went in. She's screaming stuff we can't hear. No one wants to go into the water. She slides to the end of the shore ice and breaks through into the river. One of the detectives—we see him shaking his head—goes in after her. Another cop takes off his coat and shoes and dives in, swims for the trestle. "He's dead," Mike says. "Let's get out of here."

Next day at school we hear the story as if it's news. We're captured by the assistant principal, pressured with questions, threatened with consequences. We say nothing. Macintyre knows we know, she also knows better than to ask. Debbie is furious with me and Big Mike for vanishing. We fawn and beg. "What were we supposed to do?"

We hear it took a long time to get him out of the water. A cop boat, a diver, an ambulance. The paramedics shook their heads sadly. But at the hospital a miracle—he's alive. We hear head injury and brain damage. "No harm done then," Big Mike says. We all laugh.

Mrs. Macintyre does not think it's funny. She's upset that we don't care. We do care. But we don't know what to do about caring. We only know how to act like each other, stumped and affected; one person sneezes we're all sick, someone guffaws we fall to our knees, we only cry alone. Macintyre says "callous" and we feel bad. When she scolds us, it hurts, we're embarrassed for being baffled. She's the only teacher who isn't afraid of us, which is why we love her. But still, what are we supposed to say? Crazy Mike was crazy. He ran the trestle and fell in the water. We told him not to. The only thing we know that no one else knows is that he did it to one-up Big Mike and impress Debbie. Macintyre may know that. Debbie cries and runs from the room. Mrs. Mac lets her go.

Debbie won't talk to me and Big Mike for a few days. There are questions about detention, parents call the school: How are these kids supposed to get home? Who is responsible for them? Why is there no late bus? There is talk, rumors, possible Saturday school, and something's got to be done about that damn trestle. But soon it fades. Like all else. Teenagers, people say, trespassing, doing stupid things, no lawsuit there. We're still in detention. We're warned not to cross the trestle.

Crazy Mike never comes back to school. He becomes a legend, a miracle child, the kid who died and came back. Twenty minutes in ice water. We hear they revived him after no pulse, a doctor said heartbeat undetectable. One of those rare cases where the cold shocked his body into suspended animation, hibernation, whatever. We hear oxygen deprivation, definite brain damage. We're too old for crayons and clarity, card making with construction paper and blunt nose scissors. Edible glue will not nurture us now. That's all done. We live with kids crippled in car crashes, kids abducted, kids dying of cancer. The nuns at St. Joes would have us pray, but at public school we don't bow our heads. There is no moment of silence for Crazy Mike.

One Saturday morning, Big Mike is on his porch smoking a cigarette when a special van drives by his house and backs up to Crazy Mike's house. Big Mike gets in to see him a few days later. "He's a vegetable," Big Mike tells us. "Wears diapers and drools." Crazy Mike's mother asks him to take the whaler. She doesn't want to look at it. Her son, Michael James DiOreo, our friend Crazy Mike, will never drive anything again.

It's not the same running the trestle without him. We're not a gang anymore. I'm a third wheel now. Debbie and Mike go down under the rails to the spot. I go on alone, run a pole, walk a pole, and always looking down Ribbon Street to his house when I pass. Afraid to see him, but wanting to. The weather gets better, the days longer. It becomes clear I will, with a bit of luck and help from Mrs. Macintyre, pass on to the high school across town. I want to see him before the end of the year. His mother meets me on the porch after I knock. "I'm just passing by," I say, "last week of school now."

She nods, smiles the way she used to. "He won't know you," she says. "You may tell him who you are but mustn't push him to remember. Okay?"

"Okay."

Infinitely fascinated by an Etch-A-Sketch, he doesn't look up when I walk in. "Hi Mike," I say. He's in a big high chair with an attached table like you see at a hospital. He's twisting both white knobs at once, not conceiving vertical, not comprehending horizontal. He's happily making a scribbly mess. Happy I think, yes, that's what strikes me. The old Mike wouldn't have been amused by such a device. He wouldn't have had the patience for small knobs, such firm lineation, side to side, up and down, nothing had ever been so simple. He'd have stuttered and pulsed and sent that thing aloft. This Mike's face is pasty and unfurrowed and he's happy with the chaotic mess he's making, has made. "It's Chuck from school," I say. He looks up, smiles, goes after the Etch-A-Sketch with glee. There will be no teeth grinding here, no maniac laughter, insane grin, jittery terror.

Crazy Mike is gone now. There is left this happy highchair kid. I see he's strapped in. His mom brings snickerdoodles that sit on a plate. He doesn't look at them and the one bite I take hangs dry in my throat.

When school gets out, what detention we have left is written off, forgiven, forgotten, null and void, moot, whatever. Who cares? Detaining is done. We're gone from this place. We say goodbye to Mrs. Macintyre. She always liked us. "Take care," she says. "Be careful." Mrs. Macintyre sees the future. I'm headed for college or jail. Big Mike will drop out and be drafted. Debbie will get pregnant and marry.

Then the three of us go to summer school to make up work we didn't do while in detention. Each morning we meet at Debbie's house on the river and take Crazy Mike's whaler up to the boat launch at the County Road Bridge near the police station. We tie off and hitchhike to the high school by nine. At noon we get out and take the boat to one of the islands. Big Mike steals beer from his old man, and we spend the afternoons drinking and fishing and idling around the coast. Debbie strains her bikini straps, sunning away the summer. We don't forget about Crazy Mike, he's always with us, but walking the trestle is a thing of the past. We'll never go that way again.

Then one day coming back from doing nothing, late afternoon, as we idle the boat under County Road and come face to face for the thousandth time with the trestle, Debbie says, "Let's stop at the spot."

Mike looks at me. "Why not," I say.

"Fuck it," he says and cuts the motor and we drift

under, tie off, and climb up. The raggedy piece of cardboard, a flattened corrugated box from a moving company, is still there, smoothed and stained, the edges soft and worn. Who else knows about this place? No way to tell. Cigarette butts, beer cans, used rubbers, detritus of kids with no place to go—the river sweeps it all away.

We light up and smoke and everything is quiet but for the water whirling and pooling around the timbers. Out of sheer disinterest, Big Mike, sitting cross-legged, idly flicks his Zippo on and off to a corner of the cardboard. It's been a dry summer. It's dusk now and the dampness comes on and we're wet from splashing in and out of the boat. The cardboard corner lazily burns a fuzzy blue flame. I add a sliver of dried creosote no bigger than a toothpick, then another, Debbie adds torn bits of a Marlboro box, and we have tiny cereal-bowl-size blaze going on one corner of the cardboard. It's cozy and calming, at first. The creosote slivers burn with a delayed but urgent intensity. Once heated up they ignite hot surges of little blowtorch flames. We don't even know what creosote is. Black oily smoke gets into our lungs and burns our eyes. In the tight quarters there isn't room to maneuver and we are soon captives to the blaze, choking on fumes.

"Christ," Mike says, coughing and rearing back, trying to shove the burning cardboard away from him with his foot.

"Don't feed it!" Debbie says, waving a hand in front of her face. "It's big enough."

"I'm trying to get it away from me."

"Let it burn down," I say.

But it isn't going to burn down. Quite the opposite. The cardboard burns quickly away and the fire sits atop a creosote-soaked crosstie that runs the width of the trestle.

"Son of a bitch," Mike says, trying to rise.

The spot is tight. There isn't room for three people to stand and stamp out a fire that is doubling in size by the second. Debbie is gasping and turning away. We're fucked. No one has to say it. We aren't going to be able to put out the fire. We scramble. Debbie goes first down the timber, then Mike. I have the sudden fear that Mike will start the boat and leave me, but no, I hit the boat hard, rocking it side to side. The outboard is burping and we're moving under the trestle.

We hear the blaze overhead as we pass beneath, the popping and cracking of the creosote-treated timbers as cold air sucked from the dark water feeds the fire. It roars like air forced through bellows. Heads bowed, we clear the trestle and don't look back. We head up river as fast as the whaler will go and are soon out of ear shot and Mike turns the boat in the dark and we watch transfixed as blast furnace flames engulf the crossties at the spot in the heart of the trestle and shoot up above the steel rails already starting to glow red in the night. Heat waves and flames ripple higher than we are tall through the gaps we've spent three years skipping over. Nothing else happens. Cars don't stop on County Road, cops don't run from the station, it seems we are part of something that doesn't matter. The trestle simply burns higher, out of control, and we follow the sparks racing wildly away, brilliant now against the black sky on their way to dying out.

Leaving Venice

Dave and me were sitting in Betty's Elephant Car Café a couple years after quitting high school, couple months after Dave fled New England, couple weeks after I hitchhiked down in the dead of winter. We sat at the counter on chrome stools covered with cracked red vinyl. We weren't talking much because it was early and the night before Dave told me he was sick. Said he'd been to a doctor in Sarasota. They wanted to cut him open. To look around, they said. Nothing serious. But it sounded serious the way he said it. He wanted me to go with him to the hospital, because we were friends, because he had no one else, because he was scared. He didn't say all that but I knew.

"Dave," I said, "I'm no good at hospitals."

Behind the counter Betty, retired circus trouper, now waitress and cook, fixed us a pair of Ring Two Specials—poached eggs on wheat toast with grits and bacon for $1.45.

Dave hadn't said anything about being sick on the phone. He said he had a car-cleaning business in Venice, Florida. I was doing nothing but freezing in Boston, working shit jobs, switching roommates every month. Dave said I'd be a full partner. I pictured palm trees, girls in bikinis, large drinks with flowers in them. Turned out car cleaning wasn't big business, and Venice was a bus stop, but I didn't hold it against Dave. We'd been best friends since kindergarten.

The bell over the door sounded and two guys walked in. One tall with a handlebar mustache, the other short and rat-faced, thin skin over sharp bones. They took stools at the counter. Big guy ordered a Center Ring Scramble—three eggs with onions, black olives, and sausage mixed up in an iron skillet for $1.65. The rat-faced guy had a water. Big guy told Betty he was looking for a car wash. She glanced at Dave.

"That your van?" the big guy said to us.

I spun my stool to face the plate glass window. Parked next to Dave's van with the plastic magnetized sign on the side—Dave's Auto Detailing—was a while Buick Riviera. Big guy said his dog had been hit by a car; died on the way to the vet. He needed to have bloodstains removed from the interior.

"Is it a white interior?" Dave asked.

"It was white," big guy said.

Dave went outside with the big guy while I sat sipping coffee and eyeballing the rat-faced guy. He continuously flicked his thumb against the filter of his cigarette and glared at me. I thought I'd seen him the night before climbing out of a dumpster behind the Showfolks Lounge. There were only three bars in town and Dave and me were kicked out of two of them. Only place we could go was the Showfolks. None of the places had large drinks with flowers in them.

When Dave and the big guy came back, Dave was holding two one-hundred-dollar bills. Big guy said he'd drive the Riviera down to the shop; we could keep it overnight as long as we parked it inside. They left without eating and that was the last we saw of them.

On the way to the shop we were in high spirits holding over a month's rent on a single job so we stopped at Jax Liquors to restock the beer cooler and buy a quart of Canadian Mist. Dave said the carpet looked like burnt toast. "Had to be a big dog to produce that kind of crust," he shouted over a Bob Dylan tape. "Had to be a big gutted dog."

We howled *How does it feel...* down to Dave's shop which was an end unit in a strip of garages, an open space with water for $150 a month: cement floor, roll down door, slab of tarmac out front. It was a neighborhood of transmission joints, self-storage areas, welding shops, places vacated by people after dark. Except us. Dave pulled his van inside at night and slept in it. I had a sleeping bag and the bench seat of a Chevy pickup. We were only a block from the police station so we pulled the door down after dark and kept quiet, of walked to the Showfolks, or drove off in the van which we didn't like to do because coming and going after dark attracted attention. Dave was sure we'd be taken for burglars. Dave was also sure the landlord did not intend that these units be used as homes.

The Riviera was parked in the sun outside the shop. Blood caked on the floor in smooth cracked wafers like a dried-up mud flat. "Must have been a huge dog," Dave said. He unbolted the leather seats front and back, then pulled the carpet out. The steel floor was wet with blood. I wanted to run the hose inside the car but there was no way to drain it without a hole-boring drill so I took off my sneakers and shirt and squatted inside the shell and squeegeed the muck from side to side with a dustpan. When I had a panful I scooped it up and tossed it out the door. Dave sprayed the carpet and seats down with bleach, scrubbed with a long-handled brush, hosed a pink river down the driveway. I sloshed rinse water around inside the car and sucked it up with the wet-and-dry vacuum. We took regular cigarette breaks, sitting in our wet shorts on plastic lawn chairs with the cooler between us, listening to Dylan, chasing beer with sips from the whiskey bottle. By late afternoon the floor was clean and the carpet dried on a line strung across one side of the garage.

"Dave," I said. "There's no dog that big."

We sat watching our neighbors pull down their doors and drive off. They had homes to go to. Regular houses with porches and lawn around them and couches in the living room, homes like we'd grown up in, like we'd run away from. Closing time at the shop was hard because we had no place to go. We could head for the bar or pretend to be working late. The sun was low in the sky when we got it in our heads that it would be a great idea to drive the Riviera down to the beach. "What the hell," Dave said. "We got chairs."

So we set the cooler in the car between the lawn chairs in the front where the seat would be and Dave rolled two huge joints, locked the van inside the shop, took his box of tapes, and backed the Riviera down the driveway. Dave drove pretty well but had to take the corners real slow otherwise the chairs shifted around. He had the wheel to hang onto but I fell over backwards twice before turning my chair sideways and locking onto the door with my elbows out the window.

We drove down Main Street past the police station and the Showfolks Lounge with the music blasting through the Riviera's speakers and on out of town where there were no cars. We drove over the intercostal waterway bridge and took a dirt road through the scrub pines and palmetto bushes by the circus winter quarters to a stretch of pristine shoreline with not a person in sight. In the eighties when Venice had grown, this place became a notorious nude beach with cops dragging naked women over the sand and men without a stitch in raising their arms and screaming in protest. But when Dave and I drove between the dunes of sugar sand and sawgrass, down to the water, it was wild and unknown.

We sat on the hood with our backs to the windshield in the best part of the Florida day with the sun spreading out into the gulf and the sky in the west gone the color of pink champagne. Low waves smacked the sand over Dylan singing How does it feel into the breeze that kept the mosquitos moving and the joint burning even when we zoned out and left it burning too long between our fingers. And lions were roaring. Lions or something like lions huffed loudly over to be without a home, and we were stoned enough to wonder what they wanted. Did they roar for horse hocks or rib cages? Or did they eat some sort of Purina Lion Chow? Dave said a large part of his small intestines might have to be cut out. "What do they do with that stuff? What do hospitals do with people's parts?"

"Dave," I said, "hospitals make me sick." But he would stop talking about his small intestines and with those damn lions roaring a complete unknown all I could think about was catgut. Catgut wooden tennis rackets Dave and me used when we were kids. My dad had them in the basement. They must have been made in the forties, catgut strings and warped wooden frames. Dave and me used them in the road between our houses with no direction home until all the catgut fell away loose and broken and the shellac on the frames flaked away like old skin. Dave said chemo made all your hair fall out. Said he'd never have kids. Like a rolling stone...Dave would gather no moss.

We stayed at the beach sitting and not talking much until dark, until there was an inch of backwash left in the whiskey bottle that neither of us intended to drink but would not throw away. We smoke both joints but still had beer, which we used to try to get normal enough to drive back to the shop. We drove between the dunes with the lights off following the moonlit road. The lions were quiet now. I imagined them gnawing in wormy bones and decided right then, old friends or not, I wasn't going to any damn hospital.

We saw the winter quarters lit up like a small city a mile or two across a warzone of palmetto bushes. Reaching the main road Dave switched on the headlights and turned the car toward town. I had my chair facing the door with my arms and head out the window so I didn't see what happened, but somehow Dave lost control of his lawn chair and crashed to the floor. He held onto the wheel with one hand. The car turned sideways to the road, fishtailed hard, and the two of us, with chairs, beer cooler, and box of tapes, clattered backward. When the rear wheels hit the sandy ditch the car stalled out and came to a halt buried to the frame. The rear wheels were stuck in the ditch with the front wheels on the pavement. We crawled uphill toward the door, stashed the beer in the bushes, and walked around the car for a long time, shaking our heads, saying, if only we had front-wheel drive or a couple of stout boards and some rocks and a place to stand or a tractor with none guys and a rope. We were miles from town and nobody drove this road unless they were going to the winter quarters. There was nothing except the drawbridge, the dark pines, the low palmettos. No houses, no sounds, and no lights, except across an expanse of low scrubland, the circus gleaming in the dark like a planet.

"What we need is an elephant."

"We can walk over there," Dave said. "They've got stuff to pull us out."

"Elephants?"

"Someone should stay here," he said.

""You stay, I'll go."

"I don't even have a license," he said. "What if a cop comes?"

He held his head in his hands and walked around in the road. I wanted to bed down in a dry sandy spot and sleep, but I knew he'd start walking if I didn't, and I saw for the first time a change roll over him. Blood took leave of his face and he gripped his midsection with both arms as if to wring pain from his body like a sponge. It was at least a mile to the winter quarters. "Dave," I said, "I'll walk over there."

I began walking up the middle of the road. The bridge was a hump with a glass booth. A telephone. I thought about breaking the glass. Who would I call? The police? A tow truck? The hospital? Doctor, a man in need of surgery is stranded on the winter quarters road. Then what? Hide in the bushes and watch them carry Dave away? Again I felt the urge to hit the ditch and sleep. But I went on up the middle of the road, looking back at the white car halfway across one lane, front on the pavement, rear end buried to the frame. It was too dark to see Dave.

Past the bridge I left the road and walked on a swath of trampled sand that ran through the palmettos. I walked slowly, watching for snakes in the harsh light streaking away from the winter quarters. I came to a dirt parking lot next to a building that looked like an aircraft hangar. Behind the building was an open area the size of a football field surrounded by a chainlink fence topped with three strands of barbed wire. Low buildings, animal stalls, and aluminum trailers backed up to the fence. Farthest from the main building were two large green tents. People moved about on foot and drove strange blue vehicles pulling brightly painted wagons. I heard voices. Next to the main building was a guardhouse and gate. A short stocky figure in a guard's hat dragged one leg behind him as he paced in the road under a vapor lamp attached to a telephone pole. Later I learned this was Backdoor Jack, and had I approached him that night, things would not have worked out.

I moved away from the guardhouse, keeping to the

shadows, until I came to break in the fence behind one of the green tents. A man in coveralls rolled a wheelbarrow of steaming cannonballs across a makeshift bridge, planks over vile liquid, to a manure pile. I was no expert on crap, and not thinking clearly, I suspected whatever let loose crap of those proportions had to be big. I suspected elephants.

I slipped through the gap in the fence and followed wheelbarrow man along a hard packed path between tents. They were old damp-smelling canvas tents surrounded by trenches of seeping juice the color and consistency of used motor oil. Around front I mixed with busy people. No on challenged me. An old guy sat on an overturned bucket. I sidled up to him. He held a Coke can with both hands.

"Lookin' to get on?" he said.

"Maybe."

"Hilmer's the man."

"He around."

"Somewhere." He took a hit off the Coke can. "He's generally in motion."

This didn't seem like the guy I needed to help me get the car on the road, so I stepped inside the tent flap.

Elephants. Massive. Silent, active, and close. They were chained side by side, swinging their trunks and whipping their club-like tails, rocking their heads back and forth, lifting one foot then the other, repeating each step in turn like some demented dance born out of boredom. I saw their eyes on me, acute, not missing a beat of their dance. Then like an explosion there was in front of me a compact man wearing tight bluejeans and knee-high turquoise boots, no shirt, and teeth like Chiclets. Chiclets chewing gum right out of the box. He had bleached blonde hair flowing over his shoulders and he said "Ja? Ja! What do you want? He looked like a picture torn from a glossy magazine and tossed to the gutter. All I could think of was George Armstrong Custer.

"The guy out front." I said. "He said I might get on."

"You been on bulls?"

"Bulls?"

"We're loading out," he said. "Tell Martin to set you up." He was gone before I had a chance to say I knew Elephant Car Betty.

I cut back out through the tent flap to the bucket-sitting guy with the Coke can. "You Martin?"

"You get on?"

"I guess."

"You been on bulls?"

I shrugged, somewhat affirmatively. It took me a few hours to figure out for sure that elephants were called bulls.

"Got a hook."

"Hook?"

"How 'bout a smoke?"

"I got nothing," I said, "except a car stuck in a ditch.

He leaned so far forward I thought he would fall on his face, and he hocked a blood red glob of spit between a pair of cracked wingtips with wildly curled toes. He tipped the bucket to one side, reached underneath and brought up a bottle of Everclear, unscrewed the cap, and tipped the bottle to the Coke can. He put the bottle back and slowly stood, flatfooted and swaying, like he was riding a subway. When he had his bearings, he turned and ambled off toward one of the aluminum buildings, waving me after him with the Coke can. "You can't bring no car on the road anyway," he said.

The building was crowded with men and women packing stuff into boxes and bags, leather stuff, nylon stuff, canvas, and rubber stuff, with brass rings and silver chains, steel buckles and studded straps. Elephant stuff. Martin rummaged for a club and handed it over. "Yours while you're here," he said. "You leave you leave it." It was a sledgehammer handle wrapped with black electrical tape. Embedded in one end was a vicious looking steel hook, a bullhook.

It might have been the bullhook that began to alter things. I hadn't forgotten Dave, or my mission, but for the moment I felt swept along, as my plan began to fade as soon as I slipped through that fence. I never had a plan in my life anyway that wasn't born out of necessity or desperation. I felt as if I'd fallen wide-eyed into a fast moving river. I was buoyed up, carried off. A strange collaboration of circumstances had given me a part. Playing it seemed the only thing to do.

Outside, I wandered around carrying my bullhook, trying to look on-duty, expecting someone to tell me way to do. No one did. I rolled bulltubs to wagons. When the wagons were full and the doors clamped shut, someone roared up in one of those strange bulldog-like vehicles. "Unimugs" Martin called them. They had had heavy-duty pinhole hitches on both ends, two steering wheels, and a revolving driver's seat. Their sole function was to push or pull. They whined in extremely low gears. Dave would be duly impressed if I showed up with one of these babies. I held the tongues of the wagons for the drivers to back into and tried to catch their eye, but they backed up fast, dropped the pin into the hole without leaving their seats. One driver nodded to me so I stepped up to his steering wheel and said: "I have a problem." He roared off fast.

The center of activity was the brightly lit building across the lot. Two sliding doors big enough to roll planes through were open, and inside a jungle of ropes and cables hung from the ceiling and gray canvas bags cluttered the arena floor. People lifted, lugged, carried, pointed, yelled, pushed and pulled. Shouts rose and died. Steel poles clanged and clattered as men grimed with sweat slid them into wagons and slammed the doors. The wagons were immediately taken up by unimugs and towed around the corner and out the front gate where Backdoor Jack stood. I watched from under the seats where I wouldn't get mowed down and tried to think straight. I decided Dave should come here. We'd both work on bulls and to hell with that white car. But Dave had baggage. His van, his wet-and dry, a hospital appointment, something growing in his gut. People hustled about eyeballing me standing under the seats with a bullhook so I went back toward the elephant tent. It was close to midnight. The only person sitting was the old Coke-can guy, Martin, so I got up next to him and tried to get information. "What time do we knock off?" He stared at me through eye slits like pencil lines and took a hit off his Coke can.

The blonde guy, Hilmer, grabbed my arm. "You come here." He dragged me behind him into the tent. "Next town you see Huffy," he said. "Huffy in the pie car. Tell him you're on bulls." He took my bullhook and handed me a pitchfork and I spent the rest of the night scraping soiled straw from beneath elephants. I watched and copied the other guys. You timed your work to the elephant's dance, dodging swinging tails and trunks. When the front leg came up you grabbed a sodden forkful and backed off, then the right rear, the left front and so on. They seemed okay with me, but their eyes left no doubt: they knew I had no idea what a bull was.

Before we finished, Hilmer came in yelling. Everyone put up the forks and began unchaining feet. The chains were shackled on a rear leg and each shackle had a pin that had to be unscrewed. This happened fast with a lot of loud jabbering from Hilmer and trumpeting from the bulls. Within minutes they moved all at once out of the tent. Each delicate trunk took the tail of the one preceding it. They moved with strong shorts of breath on round padded feet and lined up facing an identical group from the adjoining tent. The men stood between them. Even Martin was on his feet, bullhook in one hand, Coke can in the other. I mimicked the other guys, trying hard not to do anything stupid in the proximity of forty loose elephants and a dozen men with clubs.

I wondered where we were all going, but it didn't occur to me until later, after I'd seen the train, that all of us—elephants and their stuff, unimugs and wagons, worlds of people, animals and things that I had no notion of but had somehow become caught up in—were leaving Venice, Florida.

Hilmer bellowed and both lines of bulls moved at once. I moved as the guys near me moved. We walked at the left hind leg. We carried our clubs prominent. The beasts were not to break the trunk-tail hookup, that was gospel; if one let go of the tail our job was to hook the inside back leg and say, Tail! If the tail wasn't picked up immediately, the role of the bullhand was to take a full roundhouse swing with the club and bury the hook in the leg. This took something more of an adjustment than I'd been able to muster that night, but luckily the beasts were compliant, they knew their role, fell readily into it, and did not test mine.

The impetus of the movement, the focal point, was Hilmer. Each man and beast watched Hilmer and he watched everyone. He moved along the line and spoke in a way I could not at first understand, spoke in what I thought was a foreign tongue, but once we'd gone through the gate, past Backdoor Jack, and out onto the same quiet sandy path I'd taken across the palmetto field, I heard what he was saying was the names of the elephants. He wasn't talking to us but to them. Moving slightly faster than the herd, he cooed the name of each beast he passed. They had regular girl names: Ellen, Jenny, Cindy. He said their names slowly and affectionately and he looked each one in the eye as if they had his personal assurance that everything was under control, that they would be fine, that there was nothing in the world to worry about. Thay reassured me too. I saw that in this world bull and bullhand were not that different, both had a place, both were taken care of. I nurtured a state of helplessness about Dave, pushing guild behind fantasy, and felt better the more confusing things became. The world had shifted and I was caught in the after wind. I went with it because it was the easiest thing to do, because it was what I always did.

The eastern sky had gone peach over the black horizon. At the rate we moved we'd pass the car in broad daylight. I could bail out of the line then. I knew that. I could stop walking, hand my bullhook to Martin as he went by, and everything would be as it was the night before. Nothing would stop the line, that much was clear. If I fell down dead they'd walk on over me. But nothing else was clear to me. I didn't want to stop. I wanted to walk to Africa. I wanted to be a bullhand whatever that meant, not on a whim but because it called out to me. A voice I didn't know, yet recognized, said go this way. And I went because I didn't want to clean bloody car floors, sleep in garages, or wait in hospitals for my friend to keel over and not get up. The problem was not the car, or even Dave. But rather, could I abandon a dying man? I felt like I could. In fact a dying man felt like the best kind to abandon. Dave would understand that. Only a captain goes down with the ship, and clearly I was no captain.

We made it onto the road as the sun broke over the tree line and the inland waterway began to steam. From the drawbridge I saw the car. The herd padded silently in pairs straight down the double yellow. As we got close to the car I hunkered tight against my bull's leg, moving with her, and as we passed I peeked back under her tail and saw Dave's face in one of the windows, his eyes wide as binocular lenses. He never saw me.

Shortly after, we turned onto a dirt road and came

upon a white train parked in the woods. Brilliant white. Freshly painted white. With large red and blue letters on the side. It sat there waiting for us. For me. I was stunned. Never in my life had I considered the idea that there was a white train in the world.

Winter

Following the lead of a burly friend, I fly to Kodiak, Alaska, to work the winter crab season. I'm thinking big money, high adventure, the chance of a being on a reality TV show. When I arrive my friend has already quit. He's gone, no one knows where. I am alone now. I'm not burly. I have seven dollars and fifty cents. Large hairy men on boat decks look down at me. "What do you want kid?" The few whiskers that pass for a beard on my face are patchy and pubescent. I end up working 12 hours a day in a shrimp cannery. The money is not big, the adventure is low. There is no TV. Kodiak is between seasons in October, shrimp to crab, fall to winter. The summer help has retreated to the lower 48. The winter crabbers are not here yet. "Why do you come now?" The cannery boss asks. "At the beginning of winter? Are you stupid? Do you know what winter is like here?"

Winter didn't scare me, or maybe it did and that's why I was there. In any case the shrimp days were numbered, boats came in light, the cannery gave days off. On one of these days I decided to climb, Pillar Hill, a small mountain that loomed over town. I was alone and there wasn't much to do except drink beer in the Anchor Bar at the base of the hill. At 1400 feet the hill wasn't daunting. It was a familiar sight from the muddy street that ran along the water in front of the cannery. The hill was grassy and round like a big-bellied guardian, an overseer, a protector that shielded us from winter coming from the North. All the weather in town was maritime. The Japanese current flowed up the long graceful arm of North America bringing warm air and tides against the south side of Kodiak Island.

The day was dry and mild enough to go without gloves and I set off at noon wearing rubber cannery boots, blue jeans, a sweatshirt. I carried no food or water. I figured I'd run up the hill and be back in an hour or two for a beer at the Anchor Bar. The way up was fun, following a random route, taking huge chops with my legs, skirting the dense alder thickets and Xmas size spruce trees. When the incline grew steeper I went to my hands and knees and pulled myself along by clumps of long wiry grass. Kodiak receded behind me, the harbor with boats sounding their horns, the cannery roofs with names painted in block letters. Two thirds of the way up, I stopped to rest and watched the town below.

The grass was a thick blanket of brownish-green blades bent over and laid flat by the wind constantly strafing the slope over the town and the harbor full of white trawlers lined up in slips and coming and going out to sea that sparkled black and silver in the sun beyond the wooded barrier islands a rifle shot away and forever across the horizon. It was quiet and serene and I heard before I felt a feathery mass whisk by my head. A dark shadow flashed on the ground in front of me and I ducked instinctively and half turned from the whoop of the wingspan, a hawk dropping down the hill. He was close enough to raise hair on the back of my neck and send a rush of heat to my face. His swooping body descended purposefully, and below him on the hillside I saw the stark-white hare moving zigzag and frantic in premature winter coat that could not hide her in the grass and dark green alder bushes. The hare was vividly exposed and the hawk was streaked and speckled like the tawny hillside colors. It must have been a young hare that didn't know enough to stay underground until the snow came. Or maybe her risk taking was unavoidable, she needed to fatten up for the coming winter, which is what the hawk was doing too.

What was I doing? Far down the hill, below the hawk and the hare, small shrimp boats pulled out of the harbor, heading south for the winter, the slips filling with heavier crab boats that would risk the Bering Sea throughout the winter crab season. I wanted to be on one of those ships, to work Alaska in January, to grow a stout winter beard like the hardy fishermen I saw on TV.

I got up and went on to the top of the hill where the land flattened out like a rounded plateau. To see the other side of the mountain I had to walk a bit. The town and harbor fell out of sight. The grass was cropped short now by the wind, the terrain rough and rocky, wiry weeds no more than six inches tall sprouted among patches of ice in shaded holes. As I crossed the dome, mountains coated with fresh snow appeared peaks-first in front of me. They rose up slowly as I moved toward them. Their size made them seem close but they were miles away across a great brown valley it would take days to cross. I stopped and stared. Now I knew why everyone called Pillar a hill. Because it was the tail end, a bump, an afterthought, a stone to trip over at the close of a massive mountain range, peak after jagged peak that is the interior of Kodiak Island. The snow-white prongs were radiant in the sun, the snow thinning out at the lower elevations to salt and pepper gray, a line that dropped each night. Within days winter would move in and turn the brown valley solid white. I squinted and shaded my eyes with my hands, the sun strong in my face, the bright peaks difficult to look at. I hadn't been around a lot of mountains. I was shocked by the force of them, existing day after day, year after year, age after age, their mere presence silent and unassuming over the interim dot of the town. I stood mesmerized while the sun dropped behind them. I'd forgotten how short the days were here. The sun rose midmorning and closed out five hours later. Winter was coming. I turned to go back down.

    The top of Pillar was so broad and wide I couldn't see over the edge at any given spot which made it hard to choose a downward path. I tried to identify the place I'd come up from but the town and cannery were obscured by the hill. Nothing seemed familiar. I figured it didn't matter, down was down, and I committed to a route based on speculation. The grade was gradual at first, but once I was exposed on the face of the hill the slope became steep, the terrain wet and slippery in the shade. The sky was still blue but the sun was down behind me. There was a chilly dampness in the air. The grassy hillside I'd ascended was gone. I sidestepped down a sharp incline through a high wall of dense alder bushes, rappelling down the hill with branches tearing the skin from my hands. The bushes gave me something to hold onto but they also blocked my view of the town below. The footing was treacherous, the ground soft, uneven, and the undergrowth dense with ferns. I couldn't see my feet. More than once I felt the warning of an ankle twist, the possibility of a broken leg, or a wrenched knee which would have made the decent impossible. I felt my way down, pushing branches aside and holding on. My boss at the cannery had been attacked by a bear in exactly this situation, steep incline, high alder bushes, couldn't see anything and he walked onto a bear. They are still active in October, fattening up for the winter. Soon it would be dark and I began to consider how I'd survive a night on Pillar Hill. I'd need to burrow in, like an animal in a den, wrap myself in the long grass perhaps, curl under a bush to keep from the elements.

The panic of exposure loosened my concentration. At one point I slipped out of control three or four feet before catching a branch. I paused, hot, sweaty, thirsty, and noticed the ocean was easier to see, the harbor visible. That's good, I reasoned, water meant down. But I wasn't anywhere near down. Yet the bushes seemed to thin out in front of me. I felt air moving on my face, cooler, breezy ocean air that seemed to come from far off. I slipped a few steps further, felt the ground give way beneath me, and I collapsed clawing at the undergrowth. My feet were out over open air. I understood exactly where I was. The rock quarry. Maybe three-quarters of a mile from the cannery, on the road leading out of town, was a place they'd been excavating with heavy equipment and dynamite. This route I'd chosen to descend was precisely over the immense gouge they'd been blasting from the hill. I clutched the ground over a five-hundred foot drop into a stony quarry.

I pressed against the earth, pulling myself along by knots of grass and weeds, worming my way up. I did this gingerly because I had a picture in my mind of the quarry. They excavated high up, but also into the side of the hill. I crawled close to the edge on a thin crust of topsoil and bushes of indeterminable thickness. How much would the land bear? Would it hold me or let me go?

After maybe thirty minutes crawling away from the abyss I rose and began traversing along the top of the quarry toward the cannery. It was getting dark and I really needed water, but at least now I knew where I was. I cursed my stupidity and my cheap rubber cannery boots which were not made for the steep terrain. Since coming to Kodiak I'd been harboring Alaska-size ideas. I'd been thinking carnivorously for weeks. I'd recently bought a large-bore rifle. I was thinking kill, skin, live off the land. I was thinking a day-off jaunt up Pillar Hill. On the mainland they laugh at greenhorns from the lower-forty-eight trying to jog up Mount McKinley in tennis shoes. Strangely they often made it—a mountain that has killed world-class climbers. Mountain or molehill seems to make little difference in Alaska. Both will kill you. Below me I saw lights coming on in town. I saw the cannery where I worked, even the window of my own room in the bunkhouse. The Anchor Bar was busy—the thought of a cold beer brought tears to my eyes—patrons walking in and out, people going to eat, to a movie. They'd never see me. No one would be looking up here. I could fall down right here and never be found. I'd be scavenger food, fertilizer, spring fodder as winter folded over me. How silly is that? Stranded on Pillar Hill 500 feet above town—comfort and safety within view, and I could die here studying the indifference.

And I never finished the hare's story. How the little white bunny spun and wheeled, wildly exposed on the hillside. How the hawk banked into turns like a fighter jet following the erratic path of the hare who knew just where and when to change direction in the thick prickly-bush cover that the bird could not fly into. The hare raced from one bush to the next but seemed to have no burrow to retreat to, no fallback position; it was move fast or die. The hawk followed fast and frantic. Once the predator dropped like an arrow point flipping the hare off his feet, surely doomed I thought and cringed against a red explosion and the quiet dripping retreat of the bird. But it didn't happen. To my surprise the hare vanished into the hill somehow, patient and breathing hard underground, or inside a tunnel-like grass igloo. The hawk flew back and forth, puzzled, and then reluctantly drifted down the coast toward the snow-covered mountains. Winter would come.

Motion Sickness

"It is the unforeseen upon which we must calculate most largely." Edgar Allan Poe

Our long weekend to the coast in October, a rented beach cottage, a fall break from school, is disrupted by a recent hurricane. The cottage owner says there's been flooding, we won't be able to use the washing machine. "We could postpone," I say to Katherine. She sits upright at the piano in our living room, hands paused over the keys.

"Stick to the plan," she says. "We'll take your car."

"My car?"

"We took mine last time."

"My car, with the dog?"

"What about it?"

"Oh, nothing." But last time was a concert in Philly. Katherine is a composer. And we didn't take the dog to the city. So this trip seems, to me at least, different.

"What's the difference? Does it matter? If it matters we can take my car."

"No, no. It doesn't matter. I like to drive anyway."

"You don't want me driving your car?"

"I didn't say that. I usually drive is all. You're better at navigating. I'm not a good navigator, I mean. Right?" She flashes me a squinty-eye look, evaluating, measuring, slowly settles her hands to the keys, one note, ping, another, pong. The thing about the dog, I hate to say it, is puke. Her dog, Lila, gets carsick, especially in the mountains. You can't get to the coast from where we live without crossing the Appalachian Mountains. So there is that to squint about, to consider, to mull over, the mountains and the puking.

And the other thing is cars. Mine is new, Katherine's less new. They are both suitable vehicles. Subaru the two of them. Mine has fewer miles on it. But that isn't the thing. Okay, maybe that's part of the thing. The thing is we're grad students. We share rent but pay for our own cars, gas, upkeep, so when we go on trips for rest and relaxation the equitable nature of our relationship is paramount. We work on campus, Katherine in the music department, myself an MBA candidate, so a car is a big thing to buy and maintain. One must be mindful of the miles, wear and tear, and her car is more torn up than mine. But that isn't the thing either. The thing is sharing, taking turns, fairness, and possibly dog puke. Things unspoken because neither of us wants to be seen as petty.

"Then it's settled," I say.

I fold down the back seat in my vehicle, coat the space with rugs and blankets and plastic sheeting, and with the dog installed among the beach chairs and sleeping bags, we set off.

I have the back covered with triple-layer puke protection. But Lila, a shelter-rescued hound, she really likes us. Not uncommon. Dogs in cars mostly resent being in the back. Mostly they want to sit up front. Everyone else is up front, all the important people, the driver, the navigator. Up front is the place to be. I don't like being a passenger in a car at all, front or back. I always drive because everyone else's driving makes me sick. Lila and I have that in common. I too, am prone to motion sickness. I too, like to sit up front, nose to the windshield, sniffing out the incoming. Because that is the future and looking forward seems like the thing to do. Especially if you are upset about present stomach churning, as Lila is, stuck in the back with her head hanging over the seat. She hates car trips. She'd rather be home with her dog sitter and her doggie door so she can zip out into her own backyard and roll in her familiar grass and romp with the birds and squirrels. And who can blame her?

When I was a kid I hated car trips too, for the same reason—motion sickness. Subject to it my whole life. Not behind the wheel; drivers don't get sick. A driver can anticipate. A strategy for passengers prone to car sickness is to do everything the driver does. I mention this to Lila. "Li," I shout, "pretend you're driving, you won't get sick." I show her how to hold the wheel, elbows out, ten and two, check the mirror, honk the horn. She gives me that sidelong look dogs do when they think you're nuts. Humans are crazy she thinks emitting a hopeless sigh.

Heavy into the mountains, the road winding around, up and down—it's too much for her. She lets loose. And when she does, not all the upchuck ends up on the triple layer protective barrier. A substantial portion shoots over the seatback, filling the cup holder, running down the crack onto the floor carpet.

It's not a surprise. I knew Lila would puke. It doesn't upset me. But Katherine, well, she had hope. She's a hopeful person, more so than myself I think, she's a gifted musician, faithfully committed to touching out notes in sound-proof booths. She'd given the dog Dramamine, she'd prepared, she planned on Lila not puking. I was ready for it and calmly pull onto a gravel strip bordering the steep road.

Katherine is distraught. "I'm sorry. We should have taken my car."

"It's okay, Kate," I say. "I don't care."

"Oh, I'm so sorry."

"Forget about it. We knew it was going to happen. Get the towels. I'll walk her around."

On the leash, up and down alongside the road, we walk. We're deep in the Monongahela National Forest, the fall leaves in full-flight, a beautiful blue-sky day, no cars in sight. The hurricane hadn't touched this area. It's quiet and serene with the sun spotting through the leaves of the trees, Lila happily sniffing and pissing everywhere. Katherine doesn't find it pleasant. She's bent over the floor, scooping and soaking up, one hand holding her hair from the partially digested dog food and stomach juice, whatever that foamy yellow stuff is that smells like garbage. "Why didn't we take my car? We should have taken my car."

"Stop worrying about it," I say. "We knew this was going to happen."

But she isn't to be dissuaded from being distraught.

She can be obsessive sometimes when caught by the unexpected. We've gone on many enjoyable trips she's planned like military incursions. But at times she gets frustrated when planet earth doesn't conform precisely to Google Earth, or when the GPS sends us astray, or when I callously drive off course asserting without a shred of factual evidence. "I think it's this way."

"Now it's going to smell," she says.

"We've got windows," I say. "It's a nice day. It could be raining."

"Well at least that's it," she says. "Lila never throws up twice."

"Right. We're home free."

"Except for the smell."

"Don't worry about the smell, it doesn't smell, we've got windows."

"We'll go to a store, I'll buy some Oxy Pet Spray, a brush and a sponge."

"You don't have to buy Oxy Pet Spray. It can wait until we get home."

"We're almost out of the mountains for sure," she says when we're rolling again.

But the mountains go on longer than expected. What goes down goes back up. And the thing is, my lead foot is no soothing salve to a stomach. "Are you getting queasy too?"

"Not at all," Katherine says. She never gets car sick. I'd have been puking for sure if I wasn't driving. And for the record, it's true, the dog never puked twice on any trip we've taken. We're almost out of the mountains too. We sense it.

"It's all downhill from here," Katherine says. "Lila never throws up twice." Right then: Barfaroo!

"Oh, shit."

"Ah well."

"I think she got your sleeping bag."

I pull over, again. Walk the dog again. This time we have a fine view of a green valley, red barn, white house, cows grazing. Lila, dejected now, tramps alongside the road above the farm, sniffing and pissing half-heartedly while Katherine goes at the mop-up again. "I'll buy you a new sleeping bag," she says, shaking it out. "I'm so sorry."

"It's washable," I say. "We'll hit a laundromat when we get there. No harm done."

"I've ruined all the beach towels now."

"Laundromat."

"Spending our holiday at the laundromat is not how—"

"It's an adventure, Kate." It's clear she is, like the dog, dejected.

A double puke is new terrain, not part of her plan. We're totally off-grid, and Katherine, well, she's a grid person, she calculates, computes, she knows notes and formulas. She likes things carried out according to melodious design, parts to whole, things played out in unison. She writes scores for symphony orchestras. You can't do that slipshod. You have to be organized, disciplined. Yet, I've seen the way she works. Weekday afternoons I walk over to the music department to find her in one of the recording booths. I see her through the window, hair tied back, eyeglasses, focused. She works on a keyboard, feeling her way along, touching out a phrase, a few notes then stop, two more then stop, stutter stepping, backing up, going on again before an array of blinking and blazing equipment: synthesizer, sequencer, sampler, a triptych of monitors. Her work, very faint, comes through the wall. Ping-ping-pong. Pong-pong-ping. Back up, start again. She's finding her way, I can see it. Exploring. When I tap on the glass she smiles, holds up one finger, I watch her finish. Pinging and ponging through the forest of possibilities.

We are off again, Lila sleeping now, exhausted from puking and the sheer anxiety of puking. "How can this happen?" Katherine says. "We gave her Dramamine."

Nobody knows why motion sickness affects some people and not others. Doctors say it's a sensory mismatch. Expectations and reality out of alignment. Our stabilizing system senses motion where there is none, senses none where there is some. That's why we get sick with our butts firmly stuck to an IMAX theater seat and also standing on the rolling deck of a fishing boat. Motion sickness is conflicted senses. A sense that makes no sense. Your eyes tell you one thing, your inner ear says another, and it's barf away.

I'm convinced Katherine doesn't get car sick because she's a planner. No matter what she does, cooking a hamburger or writing a concerto, she charts her course and does not vary. She plots and sticks. Nails the dates and times. She doesn't wander, waver, add or detract. Once she commits to an idea, it's granite. Consequently, conflicting senses don't collide within this woman. Expectations and reality stay aligned. Hope and result don't mismatch and things remain on an even keel, nothing rocks the boat. She lives on the salt flats of stability.

Faith is the thing. She believes well-made plans yield predictable and satisfactory results. I figure her inner ear is like a crystal ball; she sees a future that can't be altered because, well, it's the future. It exists as fact in spite of conflicting facts like roads not taken, decisions second guessed, options passed, minds changed.

"This is it," she says. We've dropped into the green valley and are passing the farm, the cows, the chickens. She's bent over her Google printouts, her direction sheets, her notes and maps. "We're out of the mountains, flat from here on."

She's a map person of old school variety. Rand McNally is her bible. Current issue well-worn in her lap, she consults, considers, compares it to the GPS, walks her fingers through the pages, finds her way, and becomes impatient when I suggest—nose to the windshield—a disparity between her research and incoming signs and signals from the open road. Parsing the world coming at me sometimes leads to disagreements that disrupt the equitability of our relationship. This may sound minor, but, when we are traveling at high speed in traffic and I decide based on fast-arriving intel to abruptly exit stage left, or bear right by the Burger King, when I zip tootle-loo one way or another on instinct, ignoring her carved-in-stone directions, her fingertip pressed firmly to a blue or red or black line on the Rand McNally, then, we are no longer equitably aligned. We are off charted course. And that is a sensory disruption for my dear girl, when the here-and-now isn't documented, when the maps no longer align with rolling Subaru, when the plan is thwarted, meaning no safety net, meaning before you know it, we could be—*lost*!

But, we're not lost, not yet. As we near the coast, piles of debris appear alongside the road. The hurricane came ashore just south of here. Hadn't affected us on the other side of the mountains but these folks on the coast were slammed and are still cleaning up.

Katherine insists we stop for the spray, the brush, the sponge. And when we get to the cabin major Subaru scouring and scrubbing ensues. When she's done the carpet is like new. Her hands, red-raw, smell of bleach. There isn't much you can do with a woman like this except love her. So I do. I hug her and kiss her and bring her hand cream. "To hell with the laundry," I say, "let's hit the beach." She smiles and the trauma of the trip is behind us. For the time being.

She packs the beach bag. I grab the dog leash.

Though the cottage was advertised as "ocean front" a more accurate description would be once ocean front. Once upon a time waves lapped the sand a stone's throw off the porch. But then came condos, developers paved a road, slapped up pastel towers of steel and cement and signs saying Private. This departure from detail irritates Katherine. "The website specifically said ocean front," she says. "That's what we booked, that's what it said. 'Frontage' was the word used, 'ocean frontage' and that's what we paid for."

"It's okay, Kate. It's close. Let's walk."

Front or frontage, the path to the beach is convoluted. A hand-drawn map tacked to the cottage wall showed the correct route across the road and down the sidewalk to public access. Then a few wooden steps up and over the dunes. It feels stupid since the water is a straight shot across the road from the cottage. And directly across from us there's a driveway with a duplex at the end of it and whoever lives there hadn't taken in their empty trash barrel. Everyone else had. "No one is home there," I say, "let's cut through."

"There's a sign," she say. "No Trespassing."

I don't mention it again, but for two days the trash barrel stays at the end of the driveway and the house appears vacant while we walk the correct way per instructions. It isn't far and it is nice to walk together with the dog, something we rarely do at home. The thing is, every time we leave the cottage, no matter who holds the leash, Lila pulls in the direction of the vacant house. She knows where the beach is. Dogs know, and I, too, am follow-the-nose prone, but Katherine, that isn't her way so we stick to the mandated path.

We've been together since undergrad, five years now, so I know it's hard for her to relax and any suggestion that she should increases her inability to do so. Tension builds as I tiptoe around watching her work hard to unwind. Saying 'chill out' or something makes it worse. The first night we have awkward sex like strangers, the bed narrow and the ceiling fan squeaky. The second night we don't even bother. Early morning, I walk the beach with Lila while Katherine works on her computer, doing something with a plug-in keyboard and earphones.

By Sunday morning, she's adjusted to the pace of time off, now that it's time to go home. She's up early in the kitchen with her coffee and logistical gear: Rand McNally, laptop, phone, notepad and pen—studying, evaluating, weighing options and odds, determined to find a stomach-friendly route through the mountains. "We can go north or south," she says. "There must be a way. What do you think?"

"We're going to the beach," I say. "Me and Lila."

"Good idea, you guys walk, I'll figure this out."

Hooked to the leash Lila bounds off the porch pulling hard and drags me straight across the road to the empty trash barrel where she stops to pee before the vacant house. The leash hangs loose, she gives me the sidelong look, tentative and guilty. She's laying this one on me. If I even breathe in the direction of the house she'll be at it like a shot. But no, it's already decided, and we turn toward public access.

The beach is cold and the wind blows hard turning the tops of the waves into clear silver spray in the rising sun as we go sniffing about, watching surfers in black suits out on the waves.

Back at the cottage Katherine is triumphant. "I've got it!" she says. "Look at this."

She goes over her itinerary step by step, route numbers, scenic overlooks, stop for lunch. Her plan has twists and turns, byways and highways, down and around little towns. But not up. The goal is to avoid upheaval. "There are a few choices," she says. "What do you think?" She often asks me what I think but just as surely her mind is made up.

"You're the navigator," I say.

Roadmaps are neither here nor there. Red lines to blue lines to black lines. The connection to movement is suspect.

I prefer point-nose-and-go, laden with faith that I will land someplace better than what might be conjured up using the fixed coordinates of a cartographer at Rand McNally. According to her strategic plan, we are to go down into the counties south of here, then swoop back north, and that's enough to get us packed and out the door.

Pulling away from the cottage, Lila's head hangs over the seatback, Katherine's head is buried in navigational mire.

Soon we hit snags, complications, misalignments. The road south is strewn with calamity size piles of wreckage. FEMA contractors with immense clawing and scooping contraptions work with dumpsters the size of in-ground pools full of appliances and furniture bent and twisted. Household goods pushed and piled helter-skelter into heaps. Kitchen tables, living-room sets, waterlogged mattresses bloated in the sun. Flat screens and computers crushed and flooded. High end stainless steel refrigerators, doors hanging open. Katherine peers down at her maps and up at the devastation as if there must be a correlation, some discernable sense, something to make random hurricane damage part of a logical plan.

"This is unexpected," she says.

"Looks like an Allstate commercial."

A flagman directs us through a pale beach town, condos and shops, where all greenery has been uprooted or buried by fine buff sand washed and blown from the dunes across the highway. The sand lies molded, caked in ribbed waves and eddies, tiny mockups of the wind-driven ripples that created them. The air has not dried the sand enough to take it up and send it airborne to drift like caramel-colored snow against walls and bridges. The condos have roll-down shutters but the low-lying shops on the other side of the road seem sandblasted, as if grown from a tawny desert. Some shops are still boarded with plywood while others have had their barriers torn away by the storm. Everything is plastered with the same biscuit-batter sand except the black-hole windows and doors.

A sign says coffee, and we had to pee so we pull in. The little shop has lost both front windows. "Open?" I say to the woman behind the counter.

"More so than usual," she says happily.

They have no power but they have bottled water and are firing it up on a gas grill to make rudimentary drip. "Can't use the bathroom," she says. "It's backed up."

I walk Lila behind the place away from the road so we can pee. For Katherine it's more complicated. The coffee woman says FEMA has porta potties up ahead. Good news added to the bad news about the detour. "Road's washed out," she says.

We take the coffee and go find the lineup of portables. A cop is there keeping an eye on them. "Go back to the fork," he says, "then drive west around the preserve."

"It must be this green spot on the map," Katherine says, head in the Rand McNally. "Doesn't say what it is."

"Terra incognita."

"A blue spot in the middle of a green spot,"

"It's a detour, there will be signs."

But after we take the fork and drive inland around a large brackish body of water we don't see any signs. We don't see anything but wiry wetland bushes and high water and birds. I sense Katherine getting panicky. The road has that federal highway look, like in a national park, high and dry and winding around to eventually end back where it started. She can't locate us on the map and her phone has no signal. "You can't have a detour and then drop people in the middle of nowhere," she says.

The road begins to rise and the saltmarsh smell subsides and the wetland scrub gives way to solid ground and trees. "Terra firma," I say. "We're getting someplace."

But the place we get wasn't good. The road deteriorates and cuts into the side of a slope gradually rising to the north. Far off to the west we see inland hills. The phone comes on just before we hit the town. "I think, I might see," she says, "about where we are."

On the south side of the road a river runs dangerously high. Deep water moving fast, deadly quiet. Small clapboard houses on the north side are swollen, as if pumped full, the joints straining, the edges gaping. The homes are packed solid with mud that has slid loose from the hillside and dried like cement. Whatever wasn't crushed inside the houses has been rammed out through the windows and doorways and shoved across the road through the guardrail and into the trees lining the riverbank. Couch cushions, kitchen chairs, a bicycle, are caught high up in branches like a bizarre art installation.

"God," she says. "I smell gas."

The road has been plowed of red mud. In places asphalt slabs have been upsurged and carried away, leaving deep holes in the blacktop. Telephone wires, poles knocked askew, lay scrambled in ditches. We pass a yellow CAT road grader mudded over and a heap of cars and trucks pushed together and piled off the roadway. There are no birds, no people. Nothing moves but the river.

"Don't stop," she says.

This isn't a place anyone could ever live again. Entire households are razed, garages and mobile homes are rubble. There is nothing to clean up, nothing salvageable, no one will be coming back here. The place is erased from the map.

I sense tears welling up next to me—she is staring. We're lost and tired and there is something wrong with the daylight. We experience the devastation out of proportion to our situation. Lost and loss are close on the map of emotion. We pick our way along, the road rising gradually, relatively straight. Lila sleeps in the back unconcerned. Up front we're concerned. Katherine frowns, frets. She shifts her attention between navigational aids and what's coming at us through the windshield. She blames herself. "You're not responsible for mountain ranges and hurricanes," I say.

She's silent.

We come to a T-junction and I wait, staring straight ahead at a stand of trees stripped of bark. We have no idea where we were. Whichever way we go the land has a dour basted-in-mud look. Swatches of black trees are toppled as if by the swoop of a giant hand, laid out all in one direction, an acre here an acre there, pelted down. A hurricane is a system like any other, given to patterns, paths predictable, chartable, which can be planned for. And if calamity follows cleanup is the course of action. I feel seams of tension straining across the front seat that has grown much larger, the air between us is charged, pressure building, things about to rupture.

We drive on through an abandoned land using the compass on the phone to head west and come finally to a wide crossroad intersection. A blinking red light that's not blinking, a stop-and-go juncture jammed with signs pointing north, south, east and west. It's one of those perplexing concurrency road networks where one physical road is burdened with multiple route numbers. Three concurrent routes face us heading in four different directions. A triplex times four of confusion. It's breathtaking. Or maybe I just held my breath.

That's when I heard the pages, the shredding, the thump. She's torn apart the Rand McNally, slammed it to the floor. She's in tears.

"Let's take a break," I say. "We have to pee."

I pull over and get Lila out. There are no cars, no homes. The higher elevation air has lost the sewer-gas smell. "Kate," I say, opening her door. "Get out and walk around. Stretch your legs." She cries and won't budge. This isn't like her. She's generally calm under pressure, doesn't get flustered easily. At school she deftly handles a multitude of administrative and academic tasks. "Come on," I say, "everything's fine." I reach out for her but can't get close enough with Lila on the leash pulling hard for a gooseberry bush. Nose to the ground.

"This is all my fault," she says.

"It's not your fault."

"We should have gone home through the mountains."

"We wanted to go this way."

"We're lost."

"We're not lost—Lila stop pulling!"

"We don't know where we are."

"We do know where we are, we just don't appear on those silly maps." She cries childlike tears, silent, and more heartbreaking for that, streaming and dropping off her cheeks. I reach her with one hand.
"This wasn't the plan."

"Kate, honey, look, just relax. Does there always have to be a plan?"

I shouldn't have said 'relax', she doesn't like being told how to feel. "Planning," she says, slowly, as if talking to five-year old, "is the quality separating humans and animals."

What can I say? I'm being dragged away by a dog following her nose.

Katherine isn't like this at work. It's only when we have time off, days untethered from academic tedium that she gets tense. When there is no obligation or agenda, relaxation is hard for her. And I wonder why. "I've watched the way you work," I say. "You don't plan your pieces, you pick your way through."

"That's different."

"It doesn't seem different."

At home she works the old-fashioned way, a battered upright, a batch of staff paper, a few fat pencils. But the quest is the same, mapping uncharted territory, decorating our little house with notes, knocking one down, hanging up another, sounding out the way, making something in the air like bicycles in trees. Whisper and growl, catch and sustain, ping-ping-pong, pong-pong-ping. Stop. Pick up the pencil.

Scribble little birds on wires. She once told me notes were portals, one opens another, no space between them, no crossroads.

We're tired now. Jammed up. I'm too tired not to say: "Kate, which way?"

And from my navigator: "Fuck if I know." Very unlike her, the language. Her senses are scattered, she feels the churning stomach, the bile rising, the upheaval of being unmoored. Lack of control is the ultimate misery for her. She fears the present becoming the regrettable past. We've turned many corners together, and we know the roads to come will not all be well charted. We will take them together, find the way, of that there is no doubt.

This distress she feels—anxiety about the elasticity of all possible futures, the fogged crystal ball, the conflicting facts of roads not taken, decisions second guessed, options passed—this is a different kind of motion sickness. The unplanned is a sense that won't align for her. The straight line broken, the course muddled, the blueprint corrupted. She fears breaking new snow. So maybe that's my role, point man, arrowhead, eye at the helm. Forging the way, following the nose. A symmetric sense to her contrasting sense, I'm the white space between grid lines, between the notes imprisoned on the staff. Together there will be alignment then, no sensory mismatch here, rather sensory complement, whole notes only, forms coupled, complete.

And just at that ending, shocking us out of our daze, roaring through the intersection north to south, not even thinking about stop-and-go, raising a whirlwind of promise, a fleet of power & light trucks. "Kate," I say. She perks up.

"Rescue workers." They're going fast, with a sense of purpose. We crank up the Subaru and fall into the slipstream. Keeping up with the convoy, electric, charged. Windows wide open, map pages fly. "We're pinging along now aren't we?" She gives me a smile. "Pinging and ponging our way home." Lila's head hangs over. "Li," I say. "Check it out—this is how you drive, ten and two, eyes up, nose to the road."

Still Life

"Photographers deal in things which are continually vanishing and when they have vanished there is no contrivance on earth which can make them come back." - Henri Cartier-Bresson

After I stopped taking pictures I saw the one I should not have let get away. She sat in a French restaurant I chanced into during a late afternoon break from a convention in Chicago. Seeking relief from sales-rep banter and new product orientation, I slipped between heavy curtains hung inside the glass door and saw her sitting against a wall, beneath a portrait of a young boy and his dog—a signed Cartier-Bresson print mounted in a wide creamy mat and thin black frame. The boy in the photo wore a striped shirt like a Mediterranean fisherman and held with two hands his shorthaired terrier surging forward as if to burst from the picture onto her table. The dining room was tiny with adequate, diffused lighting, and our eyes locked instantly. There was no time to duck and shy away. She wore black, bare neck strung with pearls; the wallpaper at her back was bordello-burgundy. Just above her left shoulder the portrait of the boy and dog washed with grays and blurred edges in soft rural sunlight. Of course, she was with someone; this wasn't the type of place one dines alone.

She looked exactly as she had the day we met outside a theater in college. Our eyes locked that day too. "You're that barmaid," I'd said, "from the play."

"Barmaid?" She laughed at me. "Who uses a word like barmaid?"

Four years went by in an elated gasp. Our student ghetto apartment piled with prints of her. Color, black & white, sepia toned, hand colored. Was any first love this recorded? After graduation I built portfolios, applied to RIT and Cal Tech, while she continued to barmaid in plays. I never used that word again. I never stopped shooting her, trying to capture what I felt, imagined fleeting moments, idealized expectations. People liked the work and I sold some, showed in a university gallery, and she was embarrassed. But my photos never did her justice. I was never satisfied. I clicked and clicked; thinking if I shot enough one would emerge, arrive, as strong and perfect as the way I felt about her. When she said: "Can you stop?" I couldn't. When she said: "Does everything have to be documented?" I clicked. "Recorded?" I said don't move! "Captured?" When she said she was going home to Baltimore, to think about things, it was clear she'd already thought about things. Things I missed while watching through a viewfinder.

Now I find her here, framed faultlessly behind a small round table covered with white cloth against the wine-colored wall, with the pale portrait over her shoulder, and the dog surging and the boy straining and slightly backlit strands of her hair drawn by static electricity to the velour wallpaper. A ceiling-to-floor drapery hung to her right, forming a closed vertical border, thick brocade silk tied as if at the waist with a ropy tassel, a decorative device to shield dining room from bar. Her other side was wide open—the leather bench seat running like a horizon down the wall. She formed the axis point, joining up-down and across, making the world round. It was an off-balance frame, the hanging drapery clinched in the middle formed supplementary angles intersecting the ruler line of the seat, and the dog in the photo about to spring over her shoulder, the startled boy holding him back. Why did this work? It shouldn't work. There is no "correct" unbalanced framing-structure in any textbook. This one would need its own chapter to explain, the way chemistry sometimes works without explicable logic. There is an unlikely juxtaposition, a situation, a reaction, say for instance two people meet on a sidewalk, one says an archaic word and four years goes by in the click of a shutter, then silence.

There wasn't time to think and no alternative but to approach the table. The room was tight; I turned sideways squeezing between the backs of chairs. She was locked in against the wall by the table, a white napkin tucked onto her lap, the tablecloth covering her legs. She'd just taken a sip of wine, her tongue swished in her mouth, her throat bobbed, the glass quivered as she set it down. Her companion saw or felt the shift in her demeanor—he leaned back, questioning, then his head turned, following the line of her eyes and he saw me standing next to him looking down at her. She settled back in the seat, slacked her shoulders, she opened her mouth and her hands as if to catch the sky falling. "Wow," she said. Not What or Where or Whoa—no questions, just "Wow", as in, I would never have thought…

"Hello," I said. "And yes, wow." There was a pause about as long as four years. I guess we both thought something like, how is it that you are here and I feel the need to explain? "I just happened in here," I said.

Her mouth hung open but nothing came out. Her companion said, "Us too." We too, I thought, and glanced at him, then at her. "Are you in Chicago now?"

"Well yeah," she said, "I mean, no."

The guy laughed too loud. I looked at him and knew I'd seen him before. This wasn't just any guy, this was a famous actor. He wore a blue denim jacket and a western bolo tie with a choker stone too green to be turquoise. Jade, with hand-pounded silver tips. "This is Dennis," she said to me. Then to him, "Charles is an old friend from college." She took up her napkin and dabbed her lips and looked at the wine colored stain on the napkin.

"College!" He said. We shook hands, he didn't stand. Maybe I was wrong, I didn't know any actors named Dennis.

"What are you doing, here?" She said.

"Convention," I said, shrugging my shoulders. "Coincidence, I guess."

"Weird," she said.

"I heard you were in New York."

"Yes," she said. "Are you still taking pictures?"

"Yes, well, no."

The inside pocket of my jacket held a tiny digital that

weighed almost nothing, a prototype handed to me that very afternoon, SlimShot! The camera was as small as a credit card and I wanted to take it out and shoot right away before something happened to corrupt the scene. It was the exquisitely disjointed photo that was flustering me as much as who was in it. But the scene was being corrupted as we spoke, every word drove the picture of her sitting there, balancing perfectly an off-kilter frame, further from possible capture.

"Actually, I'm in sales now."

She nodded. Not even trying to comprehend. Her companion said, "Care to join us?" He looked around, thinking I must be with someone, and moved as if to rise, meaning to join her on the bench seat which would unequivocally kill the picture, disrupt the unlikely equilibrium, and utterly ruin it.

"No, no," I said, nearly touching his shoulder. "Don't move."

He was a big man, a formidable presence; possibly I'd seen him in crime thrillers, a famous man who'd be in tabloids with women, a wealthy man with influence, the type of man they let into a place like this without a proper jacket and tie. There was no way to join them, that too would corrupt the picture, if he switched to her side, put his arm around her, got closer to her, if anything moved at all, the precise picture would vanish. It was a photo within a photo. The frame was there but failed without her to complete it, the blood-like backdrop, the little boy and dog, the silk drapery heavy with tassels, and she, a way I'd never seen her. After all the ways I'd seen her, here finally by chance, a perfect picture. A life changing picture. A picture like this might have kept me in the game, led to another, to assignments, to jobs not grounded in speculation and freelancing or the trivialities of trade shows. A shot like this would have provided the life I imagined for us when we were in college.

The waiter cut in around me and set escargot boiling in a black cauldron down in the middle of the table with two tiny forks. They meant to share.

"I'm meeting someone in the bar," I said, retreating. She stared at me, sensing the lie. "Colleagues," I said, "from the convention."

"Yes," she said, and looked down at the bubbling black snails.

"I'll stop back," I said, pointing to the bar, walking backwards, bumping chairs, hands out in front of me, as if to say, don't move. Both of them watched me go.

Behind the drapery I stood, trying to breathe. There were tall bar tables with stools, very cramped, a fat man and his wife were drunk on wine. "Try this," he said, winking at me. I was shoulder to shoulder with him. "Argentine, twenty-two bucks a bottle." He put his hand to the side of his mouth. "Better than the triple-digit French shit they sell here."

I drank right from his glass. It was good. But I needed something stronger. "Remy Martin," I said to the bartender, and recalled the word barmaid, and the theater that day, and every picture I ever took of her. I still have a portfolio in a closet behind my hang-up clothes, a box of contact sheets, books of negatives, and old blocky Nikons so outmoded now. The prints are flawed, vacant, incomplete, and nowhere near as alive as the shot sitting ten feet from me in the dining room.

I wanted that picture. I wanted her perfectly framed by geometric quirk. I wanted to capture everything about her. Even when I haven't taken a picture since she left. Even if she screamed can you stop!

Truth is, her companion was in the way. His fat cowboy head would obscure the vital camera angle. Maybe if he went to the bathroom. I'd keep an eye out, watch for my chance, maybe I'd shoot him, with a gun I mean, jump from behind the curtain brandishing the new SlimShot not even on the market yet and yell: Don't move, baby, don't move now!

I wouldn't dream of it. But of course I did dream it. And other things like it. Over and over. Over the years. "Another Remy, please."

I have dreamt of the perfect subject set into the perfect frame, the perfect love alive in the perfect life, the one that got away. Could I live now with a picture so perfect? So fragile, unstructured, dismantled, unhinged, demented, damned without reason, so easily corrupted. I don't even own a gun. Cartier-Bresson said: "To photograph is to hold one's breath, when all faculties converge to capture fleeting reality." My breath has been held too long. I let it out. Moved around the drapery. Of course they were gone.

I went to the bathroom. There were no notes on the walls, no clues. Maybe a scrap of paper slipped to the waiter? I stepped back into the dining room and drew the SlimShot. I pointed it at the wall, and clicked multiple times, once even with flash. The well-heeled patrons eyeballed me nervously. The maître d' came up behind. Touched my shoulder. "Something I can help you with, Sir?"

"Stand back!" I pointed the SlimShot at him.

I stood watching the empty frame, her ghost staining the spot on the wall, a strand of hair clinging to the wallpaper. "Sir, I don't think…" the maître d' indicated the other diners. Clearly I was not the precise complement to enhance a fine French dining experience, a signed Cartier-Bresson print, a famous actor, a one-hundred dollar bottle of wine left on their table barely touched, no phone number scrawled on a cocktail napkin, nothing left but the hollow frame, no way to record the picture it begged, no way to go back and retouch, rearrange, set new props, and shoot again. This was a found photo with a hole in it, a part that couldn't be centered, balanced, put in place. "Sir, I must insist…"

"Okay, okay. I'm moving now. I'm moving!"

On the sidewalk, under the awning, only a doorman. "Cab, sir?"

Later, at my hotel, head hung over mugs of crying beer, pondering the fleeting picture, I displayed for my colleagues the SlimShot prints. "I tested it out," I told them.

"On a blank wall?" They all laughed. "There's nothing there! You're a real ace photographer, Chuck. You missed you calling." We all laughed, me too.

I will keep these shots. Yes, I am talking to you now. I'll take an old picture of you, scan it into your new frame. When you are famous on the big screen I'll make a print matted in cream and framed in steel to hang in some sun-blasted room and past and present will meet, not randomly on a sidewalk with unlikely words, or in a fancy restaurant with strangers, but in a decisive moment clicked in the heart.

Internal Injuries

People say it can never be like the old days. "We're never going to feel like we did twenty years ago," the doctor says. Is that a professional opinion? I ask him. Or are you feeling nostalgic? He says, "Well, we'll see." I doubt that. Not at this gathering. "A party" the doctor calls it. A gathering for sure, a party maybe, partly to introduce—although the doctor doesn't say so—but that's what this get-together is doing, showcasing the new girl on the block, as people are calling her. She can hardly be called a girl, fortyish isn't girly, you might be a girl at twenty like the girls in black serving hors d'oeuvres, or at sixty like The Golden Girls on TV, but not at forty, so that's off. And we don't live on blocks. Block Island yes, some of us own homes out there, Prudence Island, Cuttyhunk, Nantucket even, never the gauche ostentation of Martha's Vineyard or, God forbid, Newport. We're New Englanders. But no way block people as in walk around the block—you try that here you'll be flattened by agog golden retrievers—or throw a block party, we don't throw anything, we're boat people who don't even throw our own lines. That is to say, some of us own boats, some of us even like boats. We pay for slips and services. We stand on the dock while shirtless college boys with stomach muscles like chainmail whip our boats in and out of the water. We're summer-home people; we like homes, plural, so we're gathered this evening at the doctor's #2 house, his #1 being in the city. This home down by the point where the ocean cuts brackish estuaries into roads and islands, rocky fingers of land forming this ocean state, Rhode Island. We're gathered with old friends, some hard to recognize right off—they blurt out their names an instant before their current faces transpose the younger ones with which we grew up. We are heavier, grayer, balder. But we're close, or were, coming from the same neighborhoods and schools during the sixties and sharing the trials of that time. We don't see each other much anymore. But this gathering is not one of those hokey reunion parties with scrawled nametags stuck to shirts of fat-men-braggarts boasting of possessions and annual income, or the most-likely-to-succeed who never did trying not to show it, or the unlikely nerd turned porn star, or the everyone-had-to-have-her prom queen bloated beyond recognition. No. We've known each other too long and too well for that. It feels more like meeting the relatives at a funeral. We stand in the doctor's backyard studying each other, (like looking in a mirror), and saying, somewhat relieved, that it cannot be like the old days. We wonder where those people went, the people we were—where did they go and how did we get here?

Except for this new girl of course, this fortyish woman the doctor has taken on since his divorce, and wants to initiate apparently—we're not sure about that. It is clear she seeks assimilation, acceptance, cementation as the-doctors-wife, part of the "we" group gathered here. She's trying hard. She's divorced too. She has a mortgage, car payment, two teenagers, a small house nowhere near the point. Her driveway is dirt. Not gravel or crushed shell or pond stones, but real honest-to-poverty dirt with ruts that bottomed her clunker before the doctor bought her the new high-riding SUV. The doctor carries her financially, "for now," he says. We think, this is not your beautiful wife… But the doctor doesn't seek song or advice. He's a doctor after all, they don't ask, they consult, mostly with themselves, sometimes with experts, he tells his mother: "Ma, I'm hosting a get-together." His mother supplies the name of her caterer but won't come to the party. She doesn't like the new girl on the block; she still talks to the beautiful ex-wife who lives in the city and who the doctor fears may crash this bash. They have two sons and he told them: Don't tell your mother! But we know they did, children incite crashes. They are jumping on a round backyard trampoline, six at a time. We stand on the stone patio watching them rocket their adolescent forms twenty feet into the air and land with bone-jarring thuds on the lawn. "If we did that we'd break both ankles," the doctor says.

"Is that a professional opinion?"

We struggle to move heavy potted plants from the patio where the band will set up. "They're stuck in beach traffic," the doctor says. The late afternoon sun is high, the backyard is full of chairs and tables, a makeshift bar under a white tent. There is a flurry of activity in the kitchen as a half dozen serving girls arrive and tie small frilly aprons over their black skirts and slip on black high-heel shoes while a fat guy in a white chef's hat dons oven mitts and heats mouth-size food lined up on steel trays. The doctor issues orders: "Everyone park in the front yard! Use the port-a-john! No tromping through the house!"

"Since when is it so complicated to have a party?" I ask him. Why not a plain and simple get-down like we used to have? Lay out the chips, let 'em stuff their faces and pour their own booze until everyone lows on down and passes out.

"We don't want that," the doctor reminds me. "You know we don't want that."

Maybe he's right. We're never going to party like we did years ago.

So the gathering proceeds. The oldest friends come early. We clique together, start drinking and watch people arrive. The new girl on the block introduces herself, infuses herself, to everyone. She's expelling enough energy to run the lights if the power goes out. The band shows up in their van, unloads on the patio facing the backyard, tunes up and disappears into the basement to smoke pot. We stand around the yard holding glasses of wine and stare at the instruments resting professionally in their stands. The drums are blue and gleaming. The girls in black begin the procession of small food on silver trays. It is entertaining to watch their wobbly heels sink into the lawn. Every mouthful comes with a lacy paper doily. The band emerges from the basement and plays placid, tinkling, background music, the drummer uses brushes. We drink and make small talk. We don't reminisce or say remember-that-time…

At some point the new girl notices we are lumped up

and not circulating. "All your old friends," she says to the doctor, "get them together for a photo."

"We don't want to be in a photo," the doctor says.

She insists we pose. "How long has it been?" She says. "How long since you guys have been together?" We don't know, we shrug and stare at her, swallow our wine. The doctor's name is Howard, mine is Charles, though everyone calls us Chuck and Howie. We are all named similarly: John, Peter, Robert, and so on. We come from a white neighborhood; nobody is named Barack, which is not our fault. We wear Dockers & boat shoes, plaid shorts & sunglasses which we refuse to remove for the photo. We hold up our wine glasses and act like we're having fun. New girl clicks a couple shots then scours the crowd for someone to snap so she can jump in and be part of the gang. We spot her longing and disperse, chuckling. We do not get into pictures with just anybody, especially a new body on the block; she is no one we know.

Things deteriorate. The sun goes down. Someone is bashing the shit out of the front door using the brass door knocker, we hear it knock-knock-knocking like a distant woodpecker, the band has cranked up and people are shouting over it but the front-door people can't figure out where to go, the house is big but still, anyone with normal hearing…well that's out.

The bargirl with the red tits has a great shirt, no that's not right, the bargirl with the great tits has a red shirt, yes— that's how distracting she is. And the shirt, red, is great too, not whorish red, somewhat classy with sugar and lace, or something resembling sugar and lace, and her skin has a golden sheen that comes in a tube, glitter cream like ground mica paste rubbed over her dark even tan. "Would you like more wine?" she says. "Would you stop taking my picture?"

Parties are all the same, people get drunk, people get bored, someone doesn't show, someone won't leave, the roast beef is good, the scallops raw, red wine is dumped on white tablecloths, the band sells CDs, so-and-so gets shit-faced and falls into the fish pond, the ex-wife doesn't show, oh, what a relief. But what are we left with? Blurry cell-phone pictures, doilies like giant snowflakes blowing across the lawn, uninvited neighbors calling with complaints, an abandoned car in the front yard, cigarette butts and hangovers.

But that's not the whole story. A party is not a story. A party is merely a scene, maybe a chapter, or a symptom, or a commencement. An event played out and paid for, or vice-versa, or both, as in paid for over and over, perpetual payment, something always owed, always missed, that which cannot be undone.

A story is also what happens before.

Before the party we were in kindergarten, our parents made us walk. "But we're 5 years old," we said. They said what parents say. "When I was your age…" So we trudged down the sidewalk to kindergarten. The doctor, Howie, led the way. In middle school our parents were ghosts surfacing at troublesome moments with unintelligible pronouncements. "You are in for it mister, you are in for a change of attitude!" What could that possibly mean? We took Drivers Ed, cars with manual gears shifted on the steering column, we rode the clutch. We tried sex and drugs. We endured algebra. a + b = b + a. How can that be? Or is it bee? As in spelling. The doctor was good at all that, he went to medical school. Some of us went to the state university, some to community college, some of us got jobs, married, divorced, we grew older.

At a party when we were sixteen the doctor's younger brother choked to death on his own vomit. We'd never heard of this mode of death later made famous by Jimi Hendrix. We knew we could OD on dope, as in take-multiple-downers-and-die, but we pictured that form of ado as portrayed in movies: skid row junkies passed out in black & white bathrooms, needle in arm, drooling mouth, blissful sleep forever. That wasn't us, we were white kids, and woefully ignorant. We swallowed drugs like soup: a few of these, a number of those, if one was good two must be better, simmer in stomach-stock of alcohol and zoom off. Pills & booze, pot & booze, powder & booze. At parties we passed fruit bowls of pills. There was no small food. No girls in black skirts, no doilies. We were not fussy, astute, or careful. Peer pressure? Forget that, we wanted to outdo each other. We ingested anything we got our underage hands on. Overdosing was an abstraction. Hadn't happened yet, so why would it? Teenage logic. We had no fear. The idea of puking to death hadn't occurred to us. We rocketed high and landed with thuds.

The parents were away, the doctor left in a position of authority over his younger brother—Crazy! Even we knew parents should not trust us. It was a warm night of dancing and decadence by the pool, the house set back from the water, a curving driveway, wide open gates, plenty of mowed lawn and barbered bushes. There were no neighbors. The place was mobbed with kids, music, and booze. The doctor's brother's name was Chris, a year younger than us. By the pool I saw Chris with the heavy keg in a bear hug, pouring beer for people through the tap hole. As usual we'd screwed up the pressure pump. We used pitchers for glasses. Later I saw him standing in the grass with a quart of vodka in his hand. We were into Collins drinks then, tall frosted glasses, sweet & sour mix, a maraschino cherry, sucking the crap through straws as if it were lemonade. Too tame for Chris that night—he'd been arguing with his girlfriend and she wasn't on the scene. I watched him take a big wallop off the vodka bottle, legs splayed for balance; he turned his face up to the night sky and howled. At some point he nudged up close to me and said: "Smoke some hash?" He hushed out the word hash as if it were a holy sacrament.

"Sure."

The doctor climbed from the pool. A joint we'd pass around, sparks popping and paper ash flying, but hash called for a sit-down somewhere. "The boathouse," Chris said. The backyard dropped off into the bay and there was a considerable boathouse. We sat on the floor of a motorboat suspended above the water, life jackets for cushions, the muted party noise as background music, and we conducted the pipe-and-lighter ritual of getting stoned on hash.

The doctor and I have discussed that night many times over the years. We recall leaving the boathouse and we are sure Chris was with us. We remember seeing his blonde head climbing out of the motorboat, so we know he didn't stay and die then. In the days that followed, when we had to put a story together, the factual version for ourselves, the survival version for parents and police, there were many disjointed scenes of Chris playing records (he loved the DJ role), Chris dancing (he loved to bebop), Chris cannonballing into the pool (showoff), Chris yelling into the phone at his girlfriend (he loved that girl), Chris sulking alone (loved her more than we knew). But not one of the dozens of kids at that party—we went over this in detail—recall seeing Chris walk back down to the boathouse.

That night got late fast. Kids left, kids stayed, couples hit the bedrooms. I was about to nod out on a poolside chaise lounge when I thought: Where the hell did Chris get to? The doctor floated in the pool on a rubber raft. "Where's your brother?" The doctor opened his eyes. White Rabbit played on the stereo. We searched the house, front porch, bushes and lawn, the garage. No Chris. Across the yard loomed the boathouse. That's where we found him. My best friend's brother, Chris Kane, flat out on his back with vomit crusted around his nose and running down his cheeks from the corners of his mouth. We tried to roust him. He was out cold. We dragged him over the gunwales of the motorboat and through the door of the boathouse. His head hung back as we carried him out onto the lawn, puke, mostly vodka and beer, ran out of his mouth and nose in oily lines and landed on my bare feet. The doctor wasn't a doctor then. He was a kid. We were all kids.

"What do we do?"

"Get him up, walk him around."

"He passed out puking."

"Wake him up."

"He won't."

"He's fucked up."

"No shit."

"Fucking lightweight."

But we knew Chris was no lightweight, none of us were lightweights, now maybe, but not then, if Chris was passed out this cold there could be a problem. We carried him hammock style—I had the feet, the doctor had the underarms—across the lawn to the pool and sloshed his head into the water and we slapped his face and shouted "Chris! Chris!" Nothing. No response. Everyone stood looking down at him. In the sickly pool light we couldn't see him turning blue. We weren't smart enough to know CPR. There was no 911 then. Someone said the word hospital, the word ambulance, and we started getting very straight very fast. Finally it was decided one of the kids with a car would drive Chris to the hospital while others cleaned up the bottles and cans and upturned glasses and ashtrays stuffed with butts and roaches and the soiled sheets with rubbers under the beds and who knows what else.

The doctor looked scared. At that point we knew we were in trouble but worried mostly about parents and cops. We had not broached the word death. Had not considered the worst. We carried Chris to the car, stretched him out on the backseat and set off for the hospital twenty minutes away. Halfway there we thought we heard hacking and gasping from the backseat. "Pull over, pull over," we yelled. "He's waking up." We hit the breakdown lane and jumped out, the interior light went on, pinkish-green juice leaked from Chris's nose and mouth. "Turn him over, turn him over," the doctor yelled. "Christ! Who put him on his back?" We stood in the breakdown lane arguing about whether Chris was waking up and should we try walking him around again or continue on to the hospital. Who knows how much time we wasted or how much was spent at the house trying to revive him or how long he was alone in the boathouse but it seemed to us later, the story rehashed over many years, there was evidence Chris was still alive in the backseat of the car. We never said that to anyone.

The ER crew took one look at Chris and started moving fast. Sit and wait they told us. We shivered in wet shorts and t-shirts, bare feet on a cold hospital floor, the driver wore blue jeans. I don't know what they thought but I still did not consider the worst. He was Chris Kane who I'd grown up with, the doctor's little brother, a year behind me in school, a kid like us—he couldn't die. But he did. He had. Exactly when we couldn't say. At some point on our watch, or alone in the boathouse, Chris had drowned in his own excess, vomit filled his air passages and lungs and leaked from his nose and mouth to the motorboat floor, to my feet on the lawn, to the backseat of the car which we smelled when we drove home well after daylight. After the police came—the cop saying: "Your friend is dead."

"He's my brother," the doctor said.

The cop had a pad and a pen. The story began.

Things we learned after the funeral: Chris had been hiding stuff. Barbiturates, probably Quaaludes, enough to kill him with the booze, were found in his body. His girlfriend had broken up with him that day and he hadn't said anything. Wallowing in embarrassing self-pity Chris took a pile of stashed pills and drowned himself in booze. His girl was on suicide watch.

Things we'll never know: When did he die? Could we have saved him if we were not warped punks on drugs? Why? Always the big question. Why did it happen? Why was Chris gone? Was it parental negligence? Teenage misadventure? Act of God? We know Chris didn't kill himself on purpose. It's possible at some messed-up moment he failed to care if he lived or died—there is always that, the reckless abandon of youth in despair—but that is not the same as suicide. That was just how we lived then.

But that's not the whole story; a story is also what happens after.

Snowflake doilies at dawn lie on the grass damp with dew. The doctor and I sit in deckchairs on the stone patio overlooking the backyard. We sip vodka from frosty glasses that have been in the freezer all night along with the bottle of Stolichnaya Elit. Overturned chairs, wine-soaked tablecloths, what's left of the makeshift bar, all wet and misty. The great red-shirt girl has gone home to her boyfriend. Our old friends have departed, some in relief, others dragged off by their wives. The cost of parties is not predicable. "My ankles won't bend," the doctor says.

"We're never going to feel like we did twenty years ago," I tell him.

"Harrumph," he says. "I have some pills."

We call him the doctor because he is one. I don't know why he is a doctor. Maybe it has something to do with his brother maybe not. He was always smart in school. He treats internal conditions at his practice in the city, goes to work when he wants. Not today. Not after a party. We're in recovery. A couple of left-over guests are sleeping in a spare room, the band is passed out in their van, a pile of teenagers lie unconscious in a heap under a plastic tarp on the trampoline. Likewise the new girl on the block. She grew tired finally, as the guests drifted off, she couldn't keep up with us but didn't want to let the doctor out of her sight so at some point she lay down with the kids on the tramp. Periodically she raises her head to make sure we are still where she last saw us sitting in the deckchairs sipping vodka at sunup.

"Want to take the boat out?" the doctor says.

"What, now?"

"Yeah, you're right."

He stares at the trampoline. New girl will get up soon, we know that. About the time the sun hits that tramp she will rise and start talking and try to put thoughts in our heads or take them away.

"I was just thinking," the doctor says.

"Yeah, I see."

"Maybe fly over to Cuttyhunk for breakfast."

When he says 'fly' he means take his boat. It's one of the new "power cats". Conservative, the doctor wouldn't own a gaudy cigarette boat, but he does entertain speed, and the twin-V-hulled catamaran is able to approach 90 mph on a calm day. Today isn't that calm. There is an offshore breeze, the sea not white-capped but still choppy. "Cleanup crew is coming at 7," he says. "We don't want to be here then."

"Take her with us?"

"She's sleeping with one eye open."

As if she knows were murmuring about her, some clinging sense, she raises her head and slides off the tramp. "We're going to Cutty for breakfast," the doctor tells her.

She frowns, not wanting to go but not wanting us off on our own either. "What about the kids?"

"They'll sleep for hours."

"Maybe I'll stay here and help clean up."

"Up to you," he says.

She doesn't like boats, or at least the doctor's boat, or at least the way he operates the boat, which is mostly airborne. He likes to hit only the tips of the waves. She knows she's coming with us, we know she's coming with us; she can't bear to be left out. It's just that neither party likes the idea. She's younger than us, and not as pretty as the doctor's ex-wife.

The doctor calls the dock and by the time we drive down there the shirtless college boys have his boat in the water. "Thanks guys," the doctor says and slips them some bills.

"See you in an hour, Speedy," one of them says. They all laugh. It's a joke. The doctor is a famous speed demon; all the dock boys are amazed at how fast he gets out to the islands and back. The doctor takes pride in this designation. He smiles, takes us slowly through the no-wake zone, one hand on the steering wheel, one resting on the throttle, barely moving, gathering his forces, turning his face to the sun just above the horizon, the cold blue morning showing warm promise. It is that one hand on the vibrating throttle that portends a warm, beautiful day. The potential is there, the doctor knows hearts will pump, blood will flow.

The new girl buckles herself into one of the leather seats and grips the armrests. The doctor drives standing up in front of his seat and I stand next to him braced against the windshield. We pull out of the harbor, the boat making low guttural mutterings as we round the breakwater and the doctor points the bow to open sea. Then he pauses, doesn't look at us, he moves the throttle back a notch, taking the engine all the way down to a point we can barely hear, barely running, the boat rocking loose in the choppy wash near the breakwater. We remove our sunglasses. New girl now has a white-knuckle grip on a chrome bar in front of her seat, her chin is pressed against her chest, and she's clenching her teeth. The doctor looks at the sun, takes a deep satisfied breath and drives the throttle all the way forward. The cat leaps like a feline launched in pursuit of prey; the boat goes straight up, completely obscuring the water, all we see is the bow pointed up into the clear blue sky as the engine roars and fires water backwards.

"WAHOO!" We scream, the doctor and me, a ritual, trying to out-scream the engine. No way. We can't hear ourselves. The engine obliterates everything except the sound of the water as the boat leaps across the top of the ocean, airborne, hitting the waves just long enough to slam, bounce, and fly. The doctor knows the currents, the way the water cuts through channels and around the islands, he keeps the bow heading straight into the oncoming waves at full velocity, his goal is to drive straight at them as hard as possible, hitting just the very tips where the whitecaps break and bounce us twisting into the air again.

New girl's jaw is chattering, I see the bones in her face vibrating, her skin is stretched back in a wind-tunnel grimace. She could use a mouth guard. The thing is you can't fight force, you can't stem forward momentum, you need to go with it, hang loose, like water over rocks, like blood pumping, bone and heart moving inside skin. I stand holding the steel edge of the windshield and when the boat flies off the top of a wave I jump a bit, trying to time it just right so my body gets taken up into the air. The doctor does it too, holding onto the steering wheel. We never know how high we're going to fly, sometimes just a foot or two, but for those few seconds we're weightless, space walking, no burdens or baggage, no past or future, we're suspended in the air without time intervening. Today the waves are perfect, or the doctor is hitting them just right, we are really flying. I jump when the boat jumps and hang onto that windshield for dear life and, god almighty, I'm looking straight down at the deck. My body is prone and parallel like a gymnast on a high bar. The wind holds me momentarily like a giant cushion. Then the boat drops, seems like forever, and we hit and bounce and I jump again even higher. "Above parallel!" I scream. No one can hear me. I can't even hear myself. But I'm screaming as loud as I can, expelling invisible unheard things. I'm higher than the windshield, looking over the doctor's head, looking down on new girl grinding her teeth. Let go here and I'd fly back over the boat, over the wake too, who knows how far back into the wash of the sea. The doctor looks up at me; he's airborne too, hanging onto the steering wheel, grinning like mad and howling into the wind, riding something we set in motion long ago and have no way to control, his hair is struck straight back, he has a look in his eye I've known our entire lives.

And then we're back. At Cuttyhunk Island a dock boy ties us off and we walk toward the little breakfast place we know. Back on land, back to earth, the ground feels unreliable. We choose our steps carefully, making sure our ankles bend. "I'm starved," the doctor says.

New girl is sweating heavily. She complains of internal injuries. "I think my spleen has moved," she says, gripping her side.

The doctor looks at her. "That's not your spleen."

"Maybe your kidneys," I say, trying to be helpful.

New girl gives me an evil look. "Someday, you guys—someone is going to get hurt."

The doctor smiles at me. "Lightweight," he says.

She says, "It's just not healthy to jostle ones innards like this."

"You'll live," the doctor says.

"That," I tell her, "is a professional opinion."

The Heartbreak Business

When my daughter went into the horse business at age six, she wisely favored the promotional side—she knew better than to follow her parents into horse racing. She's watched our daily fights and frustrations, observed our chores and misery trying to make a living running thoroughbreds around in a circle. She chose, perhaps not so wisely, to employ her little white pony, Snowy. Together they waited by the front gate of our farm in Florida, Kristen in a lawn chair, Snowy, (asleep in the sun), hooked to a lead rope. Crayola colors on white cardboard taped to the gate: See a Pony That Does Tricks!

"Ah," I said. "You're in show business." She nodded enthusiastically. "How have the audiences been?"

"Nobody yet."

I wished her luck and went into the house recalling a recent family outing to a ragtag circus, clearly the inspiration for Kristen's venture.

An hour later she still sat there. Perseverance, I thought, a good quality, but I worried. This was her first venture into the harsh business world. I didn't want her hurt. She might lose her early drive. In business timing is everything. And everyone knows: location, location, location. I went back outside. "Anyone yet?"

"No," she said. Not quite as buoyant as before, but still with a sense that if she waited long enough someone would come by. Problem is we lived on a dead end dirt road running through paddocks and pastures full of horses. There was a racetrack down the end where we, along with a few neighbors, trained our horses. Maybe ten vehicles a day went by, mostly pickup trucks or commercial vans shuttling horses to and from various racetracks. So, I feared, as a business location requiring an audience, this one was compromised. Another problem, common to the horse business, is employees. I liked Snowy, but as a "pony that does tricks" he was sorely lacking. He slept about twelve hours a day and spent the other twelve grazing and hovering over his food bowl. He was sweet as ponies go, not ornery or stubborn like some, but if he knew any tricks he kept them to himself. As a unicorn-like pet for my young daughter, Snowy was great, to rely on him as a source of income was as dubious as looking for any livelihood in horses.

Kristen has always been pragmatic, persistent, stubborn even. She sat by the gate three days in a row. It was hot. Hours went by without a car. She studied the road, puzzled. I watched from the house. Heartbreaking. I considered bribing a patron or two. Our neighbors were good sports; they had kids too and knew what it was like growing up here in the sticks among adults working twenty-four hours a day for horses. I thought I might slip them a few bucks to play the audience role. But I worried: What if someone stopped and said how much for the show? I think Kristen decided it was worth five cents. When they forked over the nickel wouldn't she be in a fix? She'd find herself looking to Snowy to bail her out, an animal ten times her weight, who surely wouldn't budge from the ground where he was sacked out in the sun. My daughter would be embarrassed. Hurt. Humiliated. Her courage and vigor would be compromised. The heart might go out of her. What of her self-esteem? And where would she find herself down the road?

When my wife and I went into the horse business we worked for a trainer named Manuel who had a stable of cheap, mostly broken-down, horses at Tampa Downs. I was new to horses. Valerie rode show horses as a child and worked as a riding instructor at a local college. She was a good rider, and good looking enough in blue jeans and tank tops to get a trainer like Manuel to hire her as an exercise rider and take me on as hotwalker, cooling out the steaming horses Val brought back from the track. At that time neither of us had been anywhere near a trained racehorse.

If we'd understood anything about the horse business we wouldn't have been working for Manuel. Location, location, location. The top barns with high class horses were located near the track, close to the kitchen and piss barn. Manuel was out by the remote parking lot. He was a former jockey who spoke English by sticking an A on the end of words like give and take, and he couldn't make a V sound, so he referred to my wife as Balerie. All morning long: "Balerie, tak-a number 9. Tak-a number 10." Manuel referred to his horses by what number stall they lived in. He had a tough little filly, number 1, who made money wining about a race a month, the other fourteen used up the money and then some. Manuel wasn't any good at training and most of his horses were ailing from various leg injuries: bucked shins, bone chips, bowed tendons. They were fit 1200-pound racing beasts, bred and trained to run, and they needed to burn pent-up rage and frustration from hanging around the stall. The only relief for those poor buggers was when I took them out to walk for twenty minutes a day. They made it count, dragging me along at the end of a lead line, bucking, kicking, fighting tooth and hoof.

One day, after a bad dry spell where the tough little filly couldn't carry the barn, feed and farrier bills piling up, Manuel came to payday empty-handed. "Balerie," he said, "I giv-a you number 14." Important decisions went through Val because she was the rider. Hotwalkers were zero in the racetrack caste system, below grooms, who were below exercise riders, who were below jockeys, below trainers, below owners, below CEOs who ran the tracks, below parimutuel officials who ran horseracing. "You lik-a number 14," Manuel said. "Take him."

We did like number 14. An endearing chestnut colt called Stanley, whatever his registered name was is lost to me now. He was cute, dorky, with a sweet disposition, liquid brown eyes. He was also physically immature so Manuel hadn't bothered breaking and training him yet. I walked Stanley last and he never gave me any trouble because he hadn't been built up physically or experienced what seems to be, (for them), the raw joy of running around the track. Stanley was, like my wife and I, like Kristen years later trying to pawn pony tricks, unseasoned, innocent, green. That was us then, young, happy, full of enthusiasm. By giving Stanley to us Manuel dismissed the money he owed us and what he would subsequently spend on a body and pedigree he had no faith in. It was a good deal for Manuel, one I'm sure he quickly forgot. For us, it was the beginning.

The plan was to "get him going" which meant the basics: walk and stop, trot and stop, canter and stop. A few figure eights, pop him over a log, and we'd have a potential show horse to sell. That was our plan. Stanley was an investment. Within a few months we'd double what Manuel owed us plus whatever we spent on feed, farrier, and shots. That was our hope. We lived in a rented house on an old watermelon farm, a paint-peeling place with ten scrub acres and what was basically a giant garage. You couldn't call it a barn; it had a dirt floor and no doors. We built a stall in one corner and Stanley settled in. We bought him grain and hay and bundles of carrots and horse toys to chew on and kick around, he seemed pleased with the arrangement and that made us happy. Happy? We couldn't believe our luck. We were in the horse business—we were thrilled.

"The horse business," is a term fraught with rumor and suspicion, fodder for ridicule and misunderstanding, or to state it plainly: ignorance. Few people know the meaning of the word thoroughbred. All animals with registers to support them from Cocker Spaniels to Guernsey Bulls are "purebred." But saying "I have a thoroughbred puppy" is wildly incorrect. Most dictionaries contain the precise definition: a breed of horse used for racing. But dictionaries also include things like "Cultivated, Aristocratic, First class."

I even saw "a person brought up refined and well-mannered." And once, incredibly, I found an entry using the word to describe "a sports car."

The word Thoroughbred is a noun. A breed of horse. Period. Like Standardbred, Appaloosa, Tennessee Walker, Morgan, Hanoverian, Paso Fino.... There are many. All with papers proving their names and pedigrees, all with advocates and detractors and clubs and bureaus and registration numbers and identification tattoos. The Thoroughbred is one of them. Regardless of what your dictionary, or your neighbor who raises angora goats says, to use the word to describe pets or perceived royal peerage, is ludicrous. If the word has any elitist purity, any nobility, any inherent lightning, it is because it designates one thing: Racehorse!

Stanley wasn't one. He was a Thoroughbred on paper, registered at the Jockey Club, a dame and sire in Kentucky, but he didn't look like a racehorse, or have the personality of one, and we didn't intend to make him into one even if we could have imagined then how to do it. We couldn't. That would come later, long after Stanley was gone.

Two decades later, in Florida, recalling my daughter failing at peddling pony tricks, I worry that she will follow us into the horse business. She's a teenager now. Our farm is the only place she's ever lived, the only place she knows. From the first weeks of her life we bundled her into our pickup before dawn and rolled a half-mile down the dirt road to the training track where she sat happily strapped into her baby seat fiddling with toys and reading books while we tacked horses and ran them around the track. We had a few mares too so we bred and took horses to the sales in Ocala. It is dark-to-dark work 365 days a year for very little fiscal reward.

Kristen doesn't know what it is like to live without horses. She has had Snowy since she was too young to ride and has kept him until now, tall for her age at sixteen, she is too big to ride him. She has other horses to ride at a show barn she frequents after school. We've kept her away from the racetrack, she's a good rider but we never let her exercise the thoroughbreds. She goes to school in the morning when we train, and lately she spends more time on her computer than on any horse. She takes them for granted, which is fine. I never wanted her in the horse business. I think it hurts her mother though. Kristen never yearned for horses like Valerie did growing up in suburbia. Her businesslike father paying for riding lessons without ever understanding the affliction someone like Val lives with. The addiction to horses that's always been with her and will never go away, that which causes her, (no matter how long she's been in the horse business), to keep certain horses around long after they have no commercial value. Pets. That's what they are to her, a source of solace and anxiety, and of marital strife, and economic disaster. But she doesn't care. For my wife, the horse business is more about horse than business.

We never intended to keep Stanley. Everything went as planned. He lived in the garage and Val schooled him over cross rails and caveletti. I did the grunt work, stall cleaning, water lugging, hotwalking. We were newly married so working together felt like a honeymoon. Stanley, our first child. We cared for him as such and he was good and cooperative, happily doing what we asked. We worked at Tampa Downs throughout that winter and when Manuel asked about Stanley we proudly said how he would soon have a happy life as a show horse in a family with a young girl perhaps, someone stricken like my wife had been, who would love him more than herself and hang the ribbons he won on the walls of her room. That is how we pictured it. That's how we planned it. And for all I know, that may be how it turned out.

That spring we followed our plan. We loaded him into a two-horse trailer, hooked it to our pickup and drove to the fairgrounds, a grassy place with trucks and trailers stopped haphazardly among tents full of temporary stalls. The day was hot and sunny. This was our first horse sale. Nothing like the sales we go to here in Ocala where waiters serve drinks and fat men puff cigars while studying sale books as horses parade in and out. This wasn't a Thoroughbred sale at all, just a country horse auction, a hodgepodge of people and horses and ponies, some wild-eyed beasts straight out of fields, matted manes and tails never touched by human hands. Some were "greenbroke," meaning you might mount and not be bucked off but they didn't steer or stop. And there were some poor old decrepit creatures no longer fit for riding that would end up in dog food cans. Meat men were here too, buying horseflesh by the pound. First we'd heard of that. There were a lot of firsts that day. Not the least of which was how proud I was of Valerie when I saw Stanley next to the other horses. I found out something about my wife. She knew what she was doing. She could make a horse stand out in a crowd. This was a good woman to be in the horse business with, to be married to.

We paid $20 to enter. Stanley was assigned a stall and a stick-on hip number. People hustled about with buckets and leadropes and flakes of hay to keep the horses distracted from the turmoil and troubling garble of the PA system. When your number was called you had to have your horse ready to go and move fast to the staging area in front of the auctioneer, a loud guy in a cowboy hat: *"Once we start there's no stoppin'—you ain't here you miss your shot—lots of horses to run thru and no time for lollygagging OK here we go hip number one..."*

We waited with Stanley. Val nitpicked him with a brush. "Give me the spray bottle," she said.

"He's perfect," I said.

"His mane sticks up. I pulled it too short."

He was spotless, mane and tail combed, hooves blackened and shining, the tack gleaming—but she needed a distraction. She jumped every time the announcer yelled for the next horse. I didn't know how this was for her. I didn't know what was about to happen. She wore her leather half-chaps and blue jeans like at the racetrack rather than her dress breeches and black riding boots as she would for a horseshow. This wasn't a horseshow-type place. When Stanley's number came up she mounted quickly and rode him to the staging area, nothing but a strip of dirt in front of a flatbed truck serving as the auctioneers stand. Potential buyers stood in a half circle. They listed Stanley as greenbroke though he was more than that. He was calm and composed. Valerie posted him over poles laid out on the ground. We had about 30 seconds to prove he rode and stopped. That's all people were interested in here, ride and stop without bucking. The auctioneer whined out his spiel: *"two two who'll give me two NOW two who'll give two-five two-five two-five NOW two-five who'll give me three three..."* No one gave three. Stanley went for $2500, which was fine. We'd achieved $500 more than we'd agreed to be happy with. We'd doubled what we had in the horse. In Stanley.

One of the auction spotters handed me a ticket and I followed Valerie and Stanley back to the stall. We were trailed by a middle-aged man, a bit of a gut on him, wearing street shoes like an office worker. At least he's not a cowboy, I thought, but not a young girl either. While Val untacked Stanley and the man stepped inside the stall. He beamed happily at Stanley, clearly enchanted with him. The man said he had young kids—I looked at Valerie and smiled. He'd recently bought a farm not far away. Said he grew up with horses, then away from them, and now he wanted to get his children into it. Reasonable, this man, likeable even. We would've felt better if we could have seen the kids, but it seemed that the second part of our plan, that Stanley would have a loving family, had come to be.

Valerie told the man more about Stanley than he probably wanted to know, and somehow, without a discernable change, the man came to be standing by Stanley and we were lodged in the doorway. We stood there long after there was nothing to say. This man, a stranger, had our horse and we had a piece of paper worth 2500 dollars. We did not know this man. Clearly he was excited, thinking maybe about his kids at home, about what they would call this horse. Stanley with his liquid brown eyes. Stanley who trusted us, oblivious, munching hay, the closest thing we had to a child, no way to say goodbye.

"Don't forget your halter," the man said.

And that was it. The shock that we would leave Stanley here and drive away with an empty trailer began in my hand with his halter and leadrope. They drove home a point like an arrow up my arm to my heart and then to that place behind my eyes. My face burned. How unprepared I was. How new and unexpected to feel this way. I was blindsided by how blind I'd been. This was, after all, our plan. A plan we worked for, a plan that turned out exactly as we hoped. We should be happy, yet, if my wife had told me she was leaving me at that moment I could not have ached more. I looked at Valerie. This was why she'd been so anxious. She'd been hurt by horses before. Her first cherished pony had died of colic when she was twelve. A subsequent horse that took her into her teens had to be sold. Things happen with animals. But for me this was a first. It wouldn't be the last time I'd cry over a horse, but that first unimaginable pain stunned me.

I don't recall saying goodbye to the man, nothing like 'good luck' or anything. I don't recall throwing my arms around Stanley. I'm sure I did. I'm sure Valerie did. We said we'd keep in touch and the man said he'd send pictures—fantasy. We never saw or heard from him again.

We maintained our composure until the truck. My wife and I opening our mouths to speak, but there were no words. When we looked at one another our eyes gave us away, and gave way. We fell together in the cab of the truck, held on, and wept. Our plan was carried out with overwhelming success. We were in the horse business—we were heartbroken.

But people say, you get used to it, right? It's a business, a way to make a buck; horses are a commodity, an article of trade, a means to an end like any other product.

It's true we've sold many horses since Stanley and some I've been happy to see go, others have been painful, and some we will never part with. Snowy is here on the farm forever. Our first race winner is here—spoiled and hanging around eating, we couldn't bear to part with him after he bowed a tendon and couldn't run anymore. His mother, one of our first mares, died of a heart attack awhile back. We sold a few mares in the nineties when the sale prices fell. The prices always fall and go back up. No one knows why. The economy they say. Or bad publicity. Depends on the Arabs, the Japanese, or whatever happens in California. There is no logical or fiscal reason why horseracing endures. There is no big money in it—that's a myth. There are only horse people, who would be horse people even if they had to pay to do it, and most do pay one way or another. We've had our share of successes and failures, winners and losers, foals born dead, yearlings that run through fences, we've had them break down at the track, or never get to the track. One of our most physically impressive horses came to nothing after three years of work and expense. We gave him away to show people. He was hard for Valerie to give up on since she named him for her dad who died that year.

The horse business is full of clichés. You quickly adopt a contrived thick-skin attitude, squinting like an early-morning clocker and saying stuff like "Well, that's the horse business." And it is. But that doesn't mean people don't cry over it. When I hear someone say it's just a way to make a buck, just a horse, there'll be another down the road, I recall an old hard-boot trainer from Kentucky. He once won eight of ten races in a single day. The reporters went nuts, a miracle they said, never been done. Certainly it was unlikely, very lucky, but typical of the beyond-belief things that happen in horseracing. The reporters were even more flabbergasted when they clambered over to the trainer's barn and found him asleep in his office chair. "What the hell," they said, "you just won eight races! Aren't you excited?"

"Well," he said. "You gotta be pretty thick-skinned in this business. I get too worked up today I'll walk out of here and never win another race."

Months later, this same trainer had the top three-year-old in the country, one for the history books, a horse to do it all, break records, make the trainer more famous than he already was. On a Saturday in May he was dressed in one of his winning-circle-trophy-accepting suits for one of horseracing's big televised events. Everyone was in place. The stands packed. The commentators spieling on possible scenarios. The bets laid down. A TV camera trained on the famous trainer. The horses tacked and fired-up were loaded into the starting gate. And the race was off. At the quarter-mile pole his horse, the solid favorite, went down as if shot in the head. There was a shocked gasp from the crowd, a breath while the caller got his bearings, and the race ran on. The trainer, this man, ran too. He didn't own the horse. It wasn't his million dollars down in the dirt. He was just the trainer. That's all he'd ever been; he came from a family of trainers. He ran from his box so fast the camera lost him for a second, then picked him up, his dark overcoat dipping fast through the crowded bleachers and cheap seats to standing-room-only by the rail. We saw him throw his binoculars off his neck, duck under the rail and cross the track even as the horses, ignored by the stunned crowd, were on the homestretch. We watched him run through the dirt and under the inner rail and across the deep infield grass still wet from morning rain. He was a portly man who wore tailored suits and soft Italian shoes. As he ran we saw him dump his wool overcoat into the grass, soon the suitcoat too hit the ground, then the silk necktie flew—he ran in his white shirt. It must have been a half mile across that infield. The race was forgotten. The TV cameras followed the white shirt, sweat-soaked now, against the green grass. It seemed to take forever. The effect was unmistakable: this was a parent running to a downed child with way too much time to think about what he would find. The horse hadn't moved. A dark mound in the dirt with the jockey withering alongside. Both ambulances raced towards them. The trainer ran on. We watched with our hands over our mouths, or on our heads, or thrust into pockets. Tickets ripped in half were cast down with curses. "Fuck," someone said. "Nothing good ever happens in this sport."

Finally, one of the mounted track stewards had the

sense, or pity, to break an inner track rail and gallop after the man. I don't know which was more painful, the loss of the horse, who was wounded irreparably, or watching the "thick-skinned" trainer run. I know which I remember. Vividly. The trail of dark coats, the white shirt against the green infield, the silk tie flying.

At sixteen, Kristen sleeps all day now that school is out, spends her nights on the computer chatting with a secretive clique of friends. She won't lift a finger around the house. Farm chores? Forget it. It's through one of these online encounters that she hooks her first job at a show barn forty minutes away, a place she's ridden often, where she has friends. A girl named Sarah, a bit older, is the manager and wants Kristen to stay there for the summer and work with her. It's a safe place, if any farm can be called safe. Show grounds for pony clubbers and their soccer moms and dads with video cameras. No thoroughbreds. Kristen and Sarah will live in a trailer and run a summer riding camp for kids. This will be good. Kristen will get riding time and the job will break her nightly computer habit. She will work hard dark to dark. The twisted anguish of being sixteen will wash out in sweat. And I'm sure the horror and tedium of manual labor will come clear. She will see how sad and frustrating horse work is. She'll be happy to return to school in the fall and plan for college. That was my plan.

After a week I drive out to see what's going on. My daughter is transformed as I hoped, she works hard, she is proven to be efficient and resourceful, and has attracted the attention of the farm owner, a famous show jumper. But—

the part I didn't expect—Kristen doesn't see the horror and tedium. She says she loves horse work. She wants to stay forever. She wants to quit school and become a trainer. Her friend feels the same. They plan to be partners breaking and training horses and taking them to the shows. I can't figure it out. They set their alarms for 5 A.M., make coffee and make up their faces, spend an hour on themselves: brushing, combing, plucking, smearing, trading tight jeans and western shirts with pearl snaps, rings, bracelets, belts of silver and turquoise, earrings, gloves, boots, hats. When they're fit for the show ring, when they could lead a TV parade they look so good, they head out into dark dusty barns to feed horses and shovel shit. It's barely daylight and there isn't another human being on the farm. My daughter for whom I had high hopes, a clean life, an education, a career with decent hours, a sedan over a pickup, seems destined to become another schmuck in the horse business. Heartbreaking.

Halfway through the summer she starts telling me about a five-year-old gelding she's been working with. Walk, trot, canter. Some flat work. Jumping in the ring. "He's level headed," she says, "and I love him." I try to ignore this because I know where it is going, and it doesn't help that he's a cute chestnut, looking a lot like our old Stanley. But can't help noticing how vibrant she becomes when she talks about him, excited and happy, vigorous and open to anything, the way I remember her for most of her life before she became a sullen teenager. "Dad, are you listening to me?" she says. "He's for sale."

"All horses are for sale," I tell her.

But this sale is imminent apparently. She says he's about to be sold up north. And what will happen to him then? He may get ogre owners, idiots, abusers. He could end up starved, or a backyard horse tied to a tree, or shuffled through a fairgrounds auction full of meat men. "This horse should not be wasted," she says. "He could be something, he has potential, he needs to go somewhere useful." By this she means he needs to go nowhere except to our farm which is already overloaded with horses.

She gets her mother on her side. "The horse does move well," Val says. "He's sound and well-schooled." I try not to fall under the spell of these words, words of hope I've heard many times from my wife, from other horse people, from myself, so many futile frustrating never-ending times. This is my child. My job is to protect her from pain and heartbreak, which she says is exactly what will happen if this horse gets sold up north. "The horse could be a project for her," Valerie says. "A few months of work, bring him along, move him up." I know, I know, I know. We will double our money and instill in Kristen a sense of commerce and responsibility. An investment in our daughter's future. A plan to get her through the teenage years. She might even use this animal to scholarship into a college riding program.

So I agree, but with mixed feelings, and conditions. "This horse will not be a pet," I tell Kristen. I am firm on this. "You will work with him, sell him, and invest the money."

She says nothing.

"Six months, maybe a year," I say. "Okay?" She knows the plan, she understands pinhooking—the system of buying to resell. I keep saying "Okay? Okay?"

When she finally responds it sounds like this: "Why would I want to do that, Dad? Why would I put all that time and work into him only to give him up?"

"Not give—"

"Doesn't matter—I'd love him by then. I love him now, that's the point."

"Selling is the point," I say. "To get something out of it. To move on."

"But why would anyone want to do that?"

"That's the business. Horse after horse, repeating the pattern, increasing profit, a process of regeneration, a stream of horses in your life."

"But I love him. How could I see him go away after all that work? All that time together? How can anyone do that?"

After twenty years in the business I must know the answer to this question. I keep insisting: "That's the horse business." I know what I'm saying is true. This is how we live; this is our life. A horse is a product to sell, a job of work, a day at the office, healthy sweat, investment and return. But my insistence is feeble. I've never wanted my daughter in the horse business. I sure don't want her to feel what we felt when we sold Stanley so long ago. She senses my weakness.

"Why?" She demands. She gets right in my face. "Why Dad? Why in the world would anyone want to do that?"

To answer honestly, I can't say. I must say, I don't know. I don't know why.

Valerie and I raise cheap horses, nothing like those running in Kentucky in May. We've never, thank God, had to run across an infield to watch a horse we'd worked with for three years receive a lethal injection on national television. At some point, a point I cannot pin down, I have come to understand that I don't have what it takes to build a successful racing stable. It's not just the injuries and deaths, or the pain of the sales, or frustrations of dashed potential, or the nonstop work coupled with economic insecurity. The truth is, I don't have the heart for it. I don't have the ability and inability to be devoted and devoured, callous and careful enough to give the horses the attention they need and care for my own heart as well. Simply put, I am not thick-skinned enough to win eight races one day and the next day stab my best horse in the heart with a syringe full of Sodium Pentobarbital. If I cannot do that, I cannot be in the racehorse business.

I think Kristen with her newfound un-enterprising inclinations gave me a way out. She planted a seed by demanding an answer to a question I'd never faced, a way to the heart of the matter; she exposed the contradiction of this life for someone like me seeking only to protect my family, and someone like my wife hopelessly afflicted, and someone like my daughter not yet scarred and burdened by horses. I needed to do something for my child here, because I worried, because I didn't want her hurt, because I wondered where she would find herself down the road. So, I went back on my word, back on my good-parenting-plan-for-the-future, on twenty years of work. I bought this horse for her to keep, this five-year-old gelding with no commercial potential, so she would never have to be thick skinned, sell her love away, so she wouldn't find herself in the heartbreak business.

Because We Are Human

"My fault, my failure, is not in the passions I have, but in my lack of control of them." Jack Kerouac

I've never taken a plane without drinking, and I've flown a lot, drunk a lot, in and out of airports, on and off planes. It's not fear of flying that turns my aerial outings into drunken debacles; it's love of drinking. A love consumed, spent, abandoned just ten days ago.

So, for a recent flight to New York with my daughter, I thought I'd buy drugs to get me through. Not recreational drugs, the medical kind: Disulfiram, commonly known (to drunks) as Antabuse. Stuff that will make you deathly ill if you drink on it. I considered it security, insurance, because I didn't want to drink, and the New York trip was to see a concert, another thing I've never done without drinking, and I've seen a lot of concerts. Some lost to blackout. A big regret is missing shows I attended: Pink Floyd, Black Sabbath, Led Zeppelin are bands I slept through after extreme drinking and never had a chance to resee—Is that a word?

React is a word, reset, redo, revisit, replace, relapse.

Even reword is a word. But not resee? To-see-again seems important enough to have a word. I'd like to, for instance, resee things I've lost while drunk, lovers, hubcaps.

So I worry. The airport, the plane, the concert, time with my daughter: How am I to bear these situations warranting drink without lapsing, or relapsing—or are they the same thing?

My friend Dave was sober nine years and ten months when he unexpectedly got bumped up to first class on a flight from Boston to Phoenix. Sounded good at first, class I mean, where fragrant Cabernet flowed freely. The bottle passed under his nose, the flight attendant set without asking a plastic wine glass on his fold-down table. I'll have just one. He drank four by the plane change in Memphis, two vodka tonics in a bar there, a bottle of Chardonnay on the second leg, and an Absolute martini straight up with a twist on the way to the rent-a-car counter from which he drove one-eye-closed onto the highway around Phoenix until he crossed the median and smashed head on into a tractor-trailer truck and didn't die. He wanted to. In the hospital he begged for death. But no. Two months shy of his 10-year chip he started over again, deeply in debt, and walking with a limp. I want to avoid such embarrassment.

I don't like bothering doctors so I ordered the insurance pills on a website called The Canadian Pharmacy which doesn't exist in Canada, or anywhere else as a standard pharmacy, rather some guy named Deepak takes my order on his computer in Punjab and noting my extra $20 for "Express Shipping" promptly engages pill presser and spoons my purchase into cellophane and shoves it into a padded envelope to wait for the postman.

Two weeks later I have the pills. I don't need 100 for a weekend trip so I repackaged a few with multivitamins, Tylenol, Advil, Flex Free for my bad knees, and hydrocodone which I have a prescription for, and two Oxycodone which I do not. I mix them together in a vial with a childproof top and carry them with my toiletries in a clear plastic bathroom bag. Nothing to hide.

At the airport I'm plunged into the deep end of sobriety, protected, insurance pills between belly and bar, between me and jovial folks swilling beer at seven in the morning, responsible adults who wouldn't normally consider such behavior socially acceptable. But at airports? We fly nervous, we're on holiday. We made it through Security! Mom and Pop suck the necks of Bud Lite bottles, two Brooks Brothers' suits trade documents over cocktails, an earnest herringbone feminist of the assistant professoriate cult sips chilled white wine, her male counterpart nurses a sweating Stella Artois. College boys pound down Coronas—well, okay, we see that anywhere. The point is, as anyone who flies regularly knows, when we leave home for the airport we leave real life behind. Concerns about jobs, bills, retirement, Junior's braces, Pop's Alzheimer's, the weedy front lawn, how to find the car in a 5000 acre parking lot, are banished and having a drink seems like a fine way to lubricate our release. An airport is a trigger, the addiction-expert word for conditions launching behavioral patterns.

The trigger for this New York trip is my daughter's birthday. She's 21 now. A legal drinker, and a semi-responsible one, but with dangerous genes. She's blood kin to a long line of drunks. Parents, grandparents, uncles and cousins. She drinks regularly and has already crashed one car and has a DUI. So there is cause for concern. But she's not at all distraught, as I am, passing the many watering holes at the airport without stopping for a nine-dollar martini, or two. On the flight she ordered a Bloody Mary mostly to show off her new-adult I.D. At the hotel she doesn't feel the urge, as I do, to beeline for the lounge. So, we might say, it is good I have her with me. But she isn't always with me.

We took a two-room suite in midtown, separate bedrooms, a common area with bathroom between, plenty of privacy. To drunks privacy is paramount. Privacy means opport-unity. I felt good on arrival. I'd made my first plane trip without alcohol. I was in a hotel room without popping a cork. I wasn't carrying booze or contriving inane tales about why I had to zip down to the lobby. Small successes spawn others. That's where "one day at a time" came from. We planned dinner and a show, father/daughter bonding, she scoured Playbill.com, secured tickets, all went well. But the next night was the concert, when one day at a time became one minute at a time.

The concert was the legendary Crossroads Guitar Festival hosted by Eric Clapton to support his drying-out facility in Antigua. Thirty of the world's finest guitar players collaborated over two nights, donating their time, five hours each night in Madison Square Garden. We sat up front in the VIP section, tickets secured months ago with much finagling and large bills. I'd been to the 2010 show in Chicago and knew it would be worth the time and money. I wanted my daughter inspired; affected by music that was not her forte. She loves Broadway musicals so we agreed to sample each other's passions. I didn't know if she'd like it, and I didn't know if I could get through these two nights without drinking or depending on the insurance pills. I had them in my pocket but held off, wanting to go it clean, by will power and good intentions. Anyone can substitute one drug for another. The pills were for emergency, for desperate measure, in case of frustration or boredom.

The Chicago show was outdoors, noon to midnight on a hot day in June. Twelve hours of nonstop music while the crowd downed gallons of beer and sweated it out en masse. Crossroads 2013 was dark and cool New York nights, reserved people in such seats, but plenty of booze flowing in spite of the show being a benefit to help drug and alcohol addicts. The VIP section had its own bar a few steps off the floor. Adjacent the restrooms. Did everyone notice? Or just we who scheme and resist. I had no idea what I would do. At times I thought without a doubt I'd sneak away from my seat. Not that I had to sneak. My daughter wasn't going to say anything if I showed up with a beer in my hand. She knew I claimed to quit drinking ten days ago. But so what? Who has not said they're quitting drinking? Some say it every hangover. Nothing was stopping me from heading to the bar, bellying up: Two shots of *Jack and a Guinness* please. I felt certain I would do it. I wanted to do it. Everyone around me was drinking. We were at a concert dammit. And I was as surprised as anyone to find after the first night that I had not done it. Back at the hotel, in bed with the TV on after midnight, ears ringing from the show, totally straight, alcohol and pill free, I was startled and pleased that I hadn't lapsed. Or is it relapsed?

When my friend Dave drank after nine years and ten months he called it "relapsing".

"But Dave," I said. "You slipped once in a decade, that's a simple lapse in judgment, a mistake, mere lousy luck in decadent first class. Now you're okay again."

"No," he said. "I've relapsed. I'm an incorrigible drunk."

He made it sound as if once the mistake is made, the weakness succumbed to, the prior venerable condition is negated. More than compromised, his initial sobriety had collapsed and could not be recouped. "I'm sure that's not true, Dave," I told him. "Seems as if credit should be given for nearly ten dry years."

"No," he said. "A house leveled in a flood can be rebuilt but it's not the same house."

"Yes," I said, "but the builder's experience will make it stronger the second time."

"You can't measure sobriety by experiences," he said. "Sobriety is an organic condition, not computable by circumstance or time."

"Then why collect the chips?"

"I didn't invent the system."

He insists he was wrong to drink excessively in the first place; that, he says, was a lapse in healthy, mature behavior. All was well and dry until the return--another re-word--to drinking. That's why, he says, after his snafu in first class he is "relapsed".

Hmmm, maybe. According to the dictionary both lapse and relapse are from the Latin root, lapsus:

1. A temporary failure; a slip.
2. A decline or fall in standards.
3. A pause in continuity.

Etymologically speaking, the distinction between lapse and relapse is hazy. Modern users embrace the idea that lapse refers to a single screw up, relapse means you've screwed up repeatedly. Dave doesn't buy it. "In medical terms," he says, "relapse is a recurrence of symptoms of a disease after a period of improvement."

"You're a doctor now?"

"I have an incurable disease," he says. "It will die when I die."

Interestingly "col-lapse" isn't on any root-word list for lapse or relapse. Collapse comes from a different, darker place, which is what I tell my friend Dave. "You didn't collapse Dave, you are not leveled like a house, you simply tripped over a bump in the road, hardly your fault given those corrupt Cab pushers in first class. You fell to a trigger. A trigger Dave." He knows the lingo, he goes to AA meetings, tries to get me to join. I went once, it was religious, people were relapsed. I didn't like it.

Collapse is what my daughter did before dawn. She'd been drinking throughout the evening, demurely, steadily, before, during and after the show. At a late-night diner I drank club soda while she had pink vodka martinis and said the show was "okay," she favored Gary Clark Jr. who played hip-hop blues. Who knew there was such a thing? Back at the hotel while climbing into bed I heard a cork pop in her room, red wine bought earlier in the day. I didn't think much of it, figured to see the bottle half gone on the nightstand in the peppered light of dawn, the TV on, dead wine staining the glass, a waste of money I thought as I drifted to sleep.

My daughter has always been a steady drinker, swaying and growing mildly louder and tetchy as her blood alcohol level rises but nothing serious, she may stumble but never falls, at 21 she holds her alcohol. People say that as if it's a good thing, a redeeming quality. The fact that she can drink more than her friends and stay vertical is considered admirable in her circle—society in general favors those who drink "responsibly". That is to say, those who hide the damage.

So I worry. Because I know if we hold our liquor well it holds us. I know because I've drank with the best of them, shot for shot with hardy partyers, whisky, rum, gin, vodka: mixing excess for fun and fellowship. But that only lasts so long. Then the Jekyll and Hyde thing starts, the blackouts, drinking banishes the steady Dr. Jekyll and the raucous Mr. Hyde emerges and the next day you must ask any friends still speaking to you what exactly went down the night before. That hasn't happened to my daughter yet which is why I was surprised, scared, startled awake at 3 A.M. by the sound of copious vomiting coming from the bathroom between our rooms.

She was on her knees and elbows, her forehead pressed to the marble floor slick with vomit. I grabbed a towel and wiped her face flushed and clammy and wet with tears. She was choking faintly between dry heaves. "Can't breathe. Can't breathe." Her head was roasting. I'd seen plenty of drunks over their limit in my life but this was something different.

There are those rare scenes that seem to speak for themselves, for us rather, in moments of upmost confusion unexpected clarity sometimes hits with subsequent shock. Such was the bathroom scene. Three sensory images converged, crashed, assaulted me with circumstance, telling the story in a flash. The broken daughter, stench of vomited alcohol, and my clear plastic bathroom bag sitting next to the sink. I kept saying, "You're sick? Really? Sick?" She couldn't speak, she gasped and barfed. But the bag! The bag was screaming. I dialed 911.

Once in high school she was charged with possession of a controlled substance. Vicodin she'd lifted from her grandmother's purse. And a couple times after that, before I bought a locking cabinet, I noticed my hydrocodone diminishing faster than I was abusing them. In our house a standard bottle of Tylenol or Advil was always waylaid to her room, always on the shopping list. So she was a confirmed drug thief. And there on the counter was my drug bag.

In the ambulance to Roosevelt hospital she admitted taking pills. "What pills?" The paramedic urged questions on her. Which pills? How many? I had them all with me except the two Oxycodone I'd flushed. In my hands I cupped the hydrocodone, the Antabuse, a bunch of multivitamins and Flex Free and assorted over-the-counters all mixed up—had to be thirty pills. I tried to count, sort, to fathom what was missing, what she took, because she was semi-conscious and not talking. The trip up 8th Avenue was like a siren wailing carnival ride with the paramedic shouting and repeating everything into one of those shoulder-stuck radios like cops have.

"WHICH PILLS?"

"HOW MANY?"

Drinking with drugs doesn't alarm me. Taking prescription drugs according to the directions is no fun. The fundamental mentality of drug abusers is chaos, loss of control, embracing the unexpected. One doesn't attain nirvana by following directions. My daughter has downed alcohol with hydrocodone, she's drunk on Oxycodone, Vicodin, Valium, Ambien, while smoking pot, who knows what else. But here I was sure she took the one thing you can absolutely not consume with alcohol without dire consequences.

In the end, at the hospital, it didn't matter what she took, the result was the same. She didn't die, but like my friend Dave she probably wished she was dead when the ER crew forced activated charcoal down her throat and started talking stomach pump.

When I was 18, I went face first through the windshield of a 1938 Dodge panel truck. A beautifully restored black beast with a psychedelic procession of the planets painted on both sides, a hippy van, mattress in the back, backlights. This was 1970. My friend Dave restored the truck which I think was a bakery delivery vehicle in its day. We rolled everywhere in that thing stoned to the gills on whatever we got our hands on. Until one night our hands landed on Quaaludes and Wild Turkey. That stopped us. Or a large oak tree did. Dave, who admitted later he was seeing quadruple, drove his antique vehicle straight into the tree. There was no safety glass in 1938. The inch-thick windshield yielded grudgingly in jagged shards that took out four of my front teeth and flattened my nose. Dave appeared uninjured so most of ER attention focused on me. I recall sitting by the nurse's station swathed in blood-soaked cotton and gauze, watching Dave standing against the wall talking on a pay phone to a mutual friend, saying, "Yeah, he's really fucked up." I must have looked it with broken teeth and nose and blood-covered shirt but I distinctly recall feeling quite lucid. Quaaludes are great pain killers and the windshield kiss had a sobering effect. I felt rather peeved at Dave who, after all had failed to keep his truck on the roadway, and was now reporting callously that I'm fucked up. Exactly at that moment, me scowling at him, he went boom-down like a sack of wet cement, just collapsed, out cold, his head bouncing high on the tile floor. The nurses cursed and ran. I couldn't help but chuckle. Right, I'm fucked up. I knew he was okay, he just passed out. Let him lie, sleep it off. But that's not how they do things at the ER. They strapped him to a gurney and shoved rubber hoses up his nose and down his throat. That woke him up. He fought like a banshee, took six guys to secure him while they pumped his stomach.

My daughter escaped such horror. They don't pump stomachs much anymore. And I emphasized her copious vomiting. "Very copious," I kept saying, sticking to medical lingo.

When they had her clear and clean a doctor with a nametag came to talk to me. "Why do you have Antabuse?"

There were no cops. Accidental poisoning they called the affair. "Has it been prescribed for you?"

"I'm an alcoholic."

What a surprise! A sentence too embarrassing to say to a room full of strangers, too horrific to admit, words never before uttered, reveal here in the Roosevelt Hospital ER to a stranger who just saved my daughter's life, that her father is a drunk.

He took it like doctors do. No big deal. "Well," he said, "prescription drugs need to be secured. They're dangerous. That's why they are prescribed."

I nodded. Thanked him.

"She'll feel exhausted now. You can take her home. Watch for respiratory difficulty, chest pain, heart palpitations."

We took a cab to the hotel. "I'm sorry," she murmured, and closed her eyes, head on my shoulder, and slept. She had no clue what had happened. Probably figured the insurance pills were something akin to other downers she'd ripped off. She was drunk, careless, not caring. There was no way she'd ever heard of Antabuse, or would think her dad would have such a thing, a drug designed to help cure drunks or kill them. Us.

I've known for some time that my daughter is one of us. I understand her case—oh yes, she has a case, she's in the Alkie group, "addictive personality" as they say, bad genes, dangerous heritage, deadly linkage. Welcome to the club. The anything-to-get-high club, the can't-stop club, the never-enough club, the chaos club. "Addictive personality" sounds positive, doesn't it? As if describing one universally loved.

But no, the love is for what will send you to the hospital, get your stomach pumped, bust your teeth off, break your bones, kill you now or then. Youthful drinking before blackouts is fun, you still look good, sleep it off, suffer the hangover. And I imagine the final dementia-ridden days in the hospice or nursing home with a pint of Old Granddad under the pillow is harmless—who would care? But middle-age alcoholism is an ugly place to be.

I'd quit drinking once before when my daughter was born. I had two jobs then, school full time, my marriage was bowing to the pressures of itself, and drinking to alleviate the stress of it all naturally added to it all. I was a father. I wanted to be aware, to do a good job, and remember it. So I stopped cold for my child. But then years later out of boredom or relief or despair—who knows why—after the divorce and my daughter was grown, I lapsed or relapsed. She's had a temporary slip, a decline in standards, a pause in continuity between her ability to succumb to getting high and the necessity to maintain. She'll treat it as a glitch, negligible, par for the course. She'll say: *So What? Chill out! I said I'm sorry!* And what am I supposed to say? Why'd you do it? Don't you know better? You're grounded? This is not TV. I know exactly why she did it, and will probably do it again, why she can't help it and I can't help her.

My friend Dave said his mother quit a quart of Jack Daniels and a pack of Camels a day—a habit she'd had for 25 years—when she learned her son had addiction trouble. He called that love. I love my daughter but her drinking doesn't have much to do with my own. I didn't quit to set an example. She doesn't look to me as a role model. She's probably irritated that I no longer buy cases of wine—something we shared, along with hangovers.

We slept through the day and the second Crossroads night started off same as the first. Passing the bar on the way in and scheming with the thirsty imp that lives inside, a beast that doesn't sleep. I'll see you in there. We'll belly up once everyone is mesmerized by music. My daughter was tired but feeling okay. She sipped from a water bottle. Likewise onstage the musicians drank only water. These were famous people. Many had histories that were public knowledge. Heroin addicts, alcoholics, cocaine freaks, and more pill addictions than I knew pills. Clapton himself has been addicted to every known substance. That of course is why we have Crossroads, which is more than a concert, it's a service sparked by one man's desire to help people with addictions.

But I wasn't thinking any of that stuff. I was there for the music. For the good time. The tickets were bought months before I decided to quit drinking. And I wasn't sure I had quit drinking. Ten days is nothing. I could lapse anytime. Not slip or fall, but intentionally leave my seat and march to the bar. Why not? People all around me had drinks. But not on stage where my attention was focused on the music and all the clear plastic Evian bottles.

That may be how I ended up back at the hotel the second night still straight, unrelapsed. I puzzled over it. Tried to isolate the decisive moment when the urge to visit the bar dissipated, when the thirsty imp nodded off. It might have been when Gregg Allman stood alone on the stage with an acoustic guitar singing Neil Young's, The

Needle and the Damage Done. It's a short powerful song that has long affected me even when I used to listen to it in my teens after injecting cocaine. Allman of course is lucky to be alive with his sobriety and new liver. So is my friend Dave. So are we all. Some of us more than others.

Back at the hotel, 3 A.M. again, my child sleeping peacefully, I realized fear had been present all weekend along with the desire for drink. Then at the moment when have-a-drink turned to no-way, the fear vanished. Fear I hadn't recognized became relief. I felt it was important to harness that moment, so it could be used in the future. Because there would come again times when fear and desire would collaborate and I would need to remember the feeling of relief and use it. I'm thinking selfishly now. I know future floods will come and this experience, this Crossroads trip, will need to be part of an insurance plan more potent than pills.

Shunning the pills was as important as shunning a drink. If I'd taken them the shifting focus of desire, from wanting a drink to not wanting a drink, the feeling of fear and relief, would not have happened. So, things worked out, crossing the road in NYC without tripping, going the distance, or at least making it to the starting line without the pills. Of course I'll keep them, locked in my medicine cabinet against a weak moment, a bump to first class, a lapse or re. You can't have too much insurance when it comes to drinking. For now we've caught the beast napping, as Gregg Allman said "nobody wants to wake that monster."

So I worry. What sustains me now, 12 days along? Not many days, a number, we count to bolster state of mind. My friend Dave is correct; we cannot measure human condition by counting days. Chips are just that. If we have to count days aren't we implying that we could stop counting? Isn't "one day at a time" pretty risky when it only takes fraction of a second to decide "bottoms up"? And then your days are numbered. I seek the day when counting won't count, when I've forgotten I ever counted, when the condition called "sober" prevails as life. There will be no lapse or relapse. Act will cancel react, set stop reset, do not redo.

I have no words or definitions of words to understand the desire to drink or the lack of it. Like fear, desire is a mystery without opposite. But it is not mysterious. There isn't anything magical about want; it is the basic human condition. I wanted to drink; now I don't. I don't know why. Why do I not know why? Because I am human and the words to explain that condition are inadequate and the days are longer without alcohol and we grow older and life is short.

Until the Morning Comes

This morning I beat the old lady next door up, which makes me happy, kick-starts the day. She's tough to beat up that one. Kind-of-a raw old lady, bare-knuckled and hunchbacked, knobby knees and elbows, leathery and walking bowl-legged with a rocking-boat gait always wearing pants and she hasn't shit to do besides beat me up most mornings. Not that I give a roly-poly. I don't lay in wait for her or set my alarm to ambush her in the dark A.M. I'm not spying on her across the way. It's just every morning when I'm standing at my kitchen window above the sink waiting for my coffee machine to kick out the java there she is across the dark gap between our houses, up, dressed and moving about her well-lighted kitchen. Her cheap-ass Mr. Coffee machine glowing, a full carafe already half down. Lit up through the kitchen windows, mine and hers, I see clearly all the mundane details of her kitchen, the paper-towel roll and the cans on the counters containing the bread and cereal grains and whatnot. I see she has a spice rack. I don't have one. I haven't even had coffee yet and she's up scrubbing her countertops with Bon Ami and pulling food from her refrigerator cooking some stew or casserole and clamping her old lady chops down on the edge of her mouth-stained coffee mug which even from this distance appears disgusting. Is anything as grubby as another person's ceramic mug used repeatedly day-in-day-out without adequate cleansing? Just rinse and swish in faucet water using maybe your fingers, sparing the Palmolive because who cares, no one else is going to use it, no one would, and you'll need it again the next morning anyway, there being no end to mornings. So there's no point in putting it into the cupboard with the other cups because that's your special mug, the chosen one treasured but shoddily cared for, a vessel not shipshape, the glaze worn off, maybe even chipped, the tainted-brown top-edge kissed with coffee-stained lips, stuck with bits of breakfast grit, and she smokes too the old lady next door so add that to the besmirched rim and nicotine-stained handle. A workhorse mug, well-used in half-daze and desperation, occupying a perpetual spot in the drying strainer or simply sitting on the counter all day next to Mr. Coffee until once again here comes the early A. M. unchecked.

 She's no old laughing lady, pretty serious this one, living alone as she does, no husband or son, and beating me up every morning wearing black rubber gloves for scrubbing pots and pans in the only light in the neighborhood at that hour besides the misty street lamps. Two bright windows facing each other like bookends across a dark divide, like plain parallel mirrors placed face-to-face, an infinite regress reflecting all the other windows windows windows windows on to infinity or back to the beginning of time or wherever those likenesses go.

    Standing at the window half asleep still without coffee—cursing this slow machine—I have not a wide perspective on our pools of light. Yellow patches seen from afar like refuge in wilderness, rectangular stamps stuck down on coal-black plains, lit-up beacons in an otherwise shadowy landscape, two blazing portals into the three-dimensional staging areas we call lives: window, kitchen, house. Little boxes pressed together and surrounded by flat black, as if two spotlights have found us in a scullery theater where we carry on unseen except maybe from the heavens, some eye in the sky watching us play our parts day-in day-out, our sedentary patches of life, I mean light, as in "Let there be…"

    What sparked that first flip of the switch? Could it have been nothing more than the need for coffee? Could this joke-on-us be nothing more than some groggy deity trying to get his blood moving? Did it all spring from mere craving? Some bored god slouching toward Mr. Coffee. Some early riser without shit to do. Who knows?

    That there may be other kitchens alive and striving this early, other coffee machines gurgling and spitting onto countertops, other cracked-glaze mugs a-steaming is of course possible. But I don't see them. I can't imagine them at this hour, we are extreme me and the old lady next door, up as early as three or four A.M. Does that creep you out? Disturb your slumber, haunt your dreams, feed you guilt? Make you uneasy knowing your neighbors are up and about, lurking in the dark obscenely caffeinated and watching while you snooze?

Edward Hopper might have found us, etched and smeared us, like his Night Shadows and Nighthawks and Night Windows we two sketched in, brushed and stroked, caught web-like within our clear frames of luminance, connected here and there and divided by our narrow way surrounded by dark, static at our sinks and scoured counters with coffee machines gasping in our kitchens full of light, I mean life.

My machine has finally spit out the java and I've filled a carefully scrubbed cup with cream which is nauseating at this hour carelessly poured sugar too granulated across the counter into the cracks next to the sink no wonder there are ants. The old lady's got a big round plate draining in the strainer now. She's eaten something apparently, moving about her kitchen, drying her hands on a dishrag. Steam coming off her stove has fogged her window slightly giving her a ghostly air. She's paid me no mind over the years. Our kitchen windows unimpeded by drapes, shades, or flipping blinds, the light spills out, as they say, splashes out onto the dark ground between us.

For a long time her window had a minor crack that grew into two cracks and recently a razor-thin triangular shape fell out and smashed on the ground beneath the sash along the stone foundation where cats sleep. The old lady has a handyman for such mishaps, a geezer who cuts grass and cleans gutters. I wonder about them since he comes and goes during the day through her back door into the kitchen as if he has a key or maybe the door is unlocked. If he stayed the night I'd miss him sneaking out in the A.M. since she usually beats me up. Who cares anyway if two old farts get it on? That is to say, I'm not going to beat myself up over it.

Nor am I responsible if she dies. I mean, I'm the only one watching, buzzed on caffeine at 3 or 4 A.M. and this morning she has arrived a bit late, or I'm a bit early. But what if she doesn't appear one day and she's not sleeping with the handyman so there is no one to discover her dead in her bed? I'd see the lack of light after daze passed, before days went by I mean. I'd see no life in her kitchen, no Mr. Coffee, the stove not steaming, the sullied mug unused in the strainer. Then what?

Only the dark mornings reveal her up and about, alive and well, scrubbing and cooking and so on. I rarely see her in the light of day, once in a while crossing the backyard from garage to kitchen door. Thirteen years the same old lady beating me up every day, thirteen years we wave, exchange fragments: I say hi, she says hi. Thirteen years goes by and that's about it and why not? What the hell am I supposed to say to an old passing lady?

It takes about three cups of coffee for daylight to emerge. Clearly and imperceptivity our lively windows pale, lose their definition, the light goes out of them, the life of our kitchens grows dim and gradually the windows turn from warm beacons of light to cold stone-gray slabs. The windowpanes invisible in the dark turn glossy and reflective in the rising dawn. Where does dark go with the coming of light? Well, it's not a mystery, a desk lamp and a globe solves that question. But along the murky path between us I feel dark fading or light evolving—there is no difference. There are bushes on my side, minor greenery, nothing but plain gray clapboard on her side and the windows losing their flame. The sky appears first, stars fading into blue over the roof of her house. There is no raging here against the dying or rising light, we stand mute watching all come and go, having one more cup of coffee for the road. The heartbeats kick up as if we may be the source of the day bled from our windows to the outside world. Morning comes on, we fade, evanescent, ephemeral. Standing still at the window over the sink by the coffee machine, my sparkling mug grown cold, the day imposes until our kitchens dwindle little by little and we disappear.

    I'm thinking, as time goes on, if I could beat her up more often, get the jump on her daily by a few minutes, hours over weeks, days over months, months over years, with plenty of caffeine to harden the arteries and stain the teeth and crack glaze on mugs, I might grow old faster, catch up to her and marry her. We could be something then, a couple joined in kitchen solitude and coffee seeped in domestic bliss, or at least life less lonely, and maybe then live on after the morning comes.

Living Among Strangers

"There were things under things, as well as things inside things."
H.D.

Dump trucks rattle up to where the asphalt ends. Men in boots go afoot into the woods carrying tripods and tool boxes. They shove wooden stakes into the sand and tie ribbons around trees. Yellow steel-jawed contraptions mouth longleaf pines and tear them roots-and-all from the earth. Palmetto bushes are bulldozed into piles and burned. Frightened displaced critters, snakes and rodents, their burrows crushed, their lives upended, scoot down tire-tread ruts into this upscale neighborhood south of Sarasota. Kids ravage the building site, finding tiger skulls, elephant tusks, bear claws. They run through the streets screaming "Dinosaur bones!"

"No," I tell them. "No prehistoric land carnivores lived in Florida. I know, children, I was a school teacher." They take a step back. "Seawater," I say, "sharks and crustaceans lived here before us."

Dewy mornings I don my Nikes and powerwalk the wide looping streets quiet before the sun clears the trees and starts the Spanish-tile rooftops a steaming. I stride unstained sidewalks, skip over crisp-edged curbstones. Fat SUVs roll by, men in suits, moms seeing kids off to school. "Morning" everyone says. "Good morning Mrs. Beamons!" I wave and say it back as if I know these people. As if I care.

Some of us in the neighborhood are retired or semi-retired. This is not one of those golf-cart villages of infirm northerners. My children want me in a place like that, my three daughters in concert like musketeers, or stooges. They say: We want you happy Mom, cared for, with likeminded people. "Like minded." What does that even mean? I have no intention of going anywhere. I do not play shuffleboard or bridge. I am not elderly. I am recently widowed. Twenty-five years I taught school up north so I know a thing or two.

I walk to the gatehouse and turn back. The gateman says "Morning Mrs. Beamon." I can't tell if he leaves the s off on purpose, like a rude student, or if he's just an ignoramus. I suspect the latter. A pudgy man wearing a polo shirt and beige shorts, he waves us in and out, a gateman without a gate, not even one of those up-and-down bars to raise and lower with some authority—he has none. He has a phone. Anything suspicious he calls the police. There has never been anything suspicious. Until now.

Now the construction comes to an end, the men in boots abandon the woods, they halt their contraptions and leave. Police tape off the site. An unmarked car shows up, detectives wearing rubber gloves. The coroner arrives, then a university specialist, a news team.

I'm not nosy. I do not meddle, snoop, or pry. I own a stately sedan with a tag that reads: MYOB. But I watch the news. I follow world events. I know where bombs regularly go off, where the hurricanes are, and naturally, I monitor the action if it occurs in my own neighborhood. Twenty-five years in middle school you acquire an instinct for intrigue, an ear for chronicle, you acclimatize inquisitiveness. I move in on the news truck. The reporter, newsperson they say now, a big-blonde-designer-suit-painted-face fresh out of journalism school faces the camera. I don't want to be called Granny and be told to shove off, step aside, go home, so I wait until they're done then sidle up to the cameraman as he loads his stuff. "Big story?"

"Big is right," he says. "Big dead body."

The nightly news shows a clip. Miss Makeup standing on our street talking to the camera. I'm behind the police tape with the neighborhood kids, grandma in pink warm-ups and jogging shoes. Gawd! I look like Richard Simmons. My flyaway hair is thinning. The report says human remains in a box, not unusual nowadays, but these are huge remains apparently, and the box is an old train car, a boxcar with giant bones inside, the whole thing buried forty years or more. The bones of a woman, they say. A huge woman, a giantess, legs like tree trunks, gorilla arms, ribcage big as a Volkswagen. Miss Makeup lays on the drama: "And who might she be? How did she get here? What will happen now? That's what folks here in Bahia Vista Estates want to know— Angela Fairchild, WFLA NEWS."

My neighbors are upset. The older people sigh and shake their blue and bald heads. The couples with kids are upwardly mobile, strident, determined. They want answers. The police won't let them near the boxcar site. The men talk night raid. They'll go with flashlights down the street to climb the new chain-link fence with the No Trespassing sign. It's their neighborhood damn it, and a darn nice one, they have a right to know. But their wives say no, let the authorities handle it, stay home where you belong.

But it's too late for that. These people left their homes in Ohio, Indiana, Michigan.... They packed their past and moved to sunny Florida. People like me and my husband who traded leftover lives for a quarter acre of sand and a kidney-shaped pool. We weren't here six months when my husband, pulling the plastic bag full of trash from the dustbin, fell dead of a heart attack. He hated it here anyway. The heat, the bugs, the sand. "Can't even grow a tomato in the yard," he used to say. I shipped him back up north to be buried. Our girls are scattered all over: New England, California, New York. As soon as their father died they started in on me to sell the house and move to assisted living. They say "come stay with us Mom." After raising three kids and god-all-too-many students, I'm going to live in a house with grandchildren? I don't think so.

After the news story appears the neighborhood expansion stalls. Whoever or whatever is in that boxcar has become a political issue. The contractors say bulldoze the giantess out of there. The coroner says that's not an option, it's a human body. The university guy says it's an archeological find. Some feminists show up and say it is not an it—*She's a woman!* The Jewish league is concerned, they heard bones, boxcar—can't be too careful.

Three days after the discovery I'm out early before the sun while the sprinklers hiss and spray in the dark. I come upon a low-slung van parked on the road where the asphalt ends. A man in jeans, hooded sweatshirt, and a pair of black engineer boots like I haven't seen since I was a teenager in the fifties, is pressed to the fence surrounding the construction site. I make an about-face in the middle of the road, he hears me and turns. He's slight and unkempt, about my age but lean and fit, he's worked outside all his life. I wonder how he's passed the gatehouse since he's clearly not a resident or construction worker, twenty-five years in school you get an eye for this sort of thing; he's in the hallway without a pass. "Morning," he says. "You're out and about early."

"You too."

"The news moves," he says. He walks over and slaps the van and I see it's loaded with bundles of the *Sarasota Herald Tribune*. "Pretty old for a paper boy ain't I?"

I smile and walk on. He laughs and leans against the van. "Have a nice day." He shows no sign of being in a hurry.

After that I notice him on and off if I am striding the streets early. He drops bundles of newspapers on corners before dawn then reconnoiters the fence at the end of the road. He's personable and in spite of a large dead body and recent police presence I feel safe in this neighborhood, or at least left-alone in dull routine. This man is a break in the monotony; he's jovial and chatty. Besides, no one else is out this early. "So what are you doing down here?" he says to me one day.

"I live here."

"You don't live here."

"You are telling me I don't live in this neighborhood? Are you crazy?"

"I'm a sixty-year old paperboy. Course I'm crazy." He laughs. I walk on.

Next day he says: "It's a winter job. I'm on the road when the good weather comes. I run concessions: snow cones, popcorn, cotton candy—like that. I build the stands, contract 'em out. Show dates, fairs, a few tent shows—not many around anymore."

In time I come to understand he's one the old Sarasota residents. He was born here at a time when train cars ran right down the middle of Main Street.

"I lived here," he says. "This was my neighborhood once," he says. "Ours," he calls it. "Before y'all came. I know who lives here for real," he says. "I know what's buried here."

"What?" I say.

"You wouldn't believe me if I told you."

"I was a school teacher," I say.

"I'll show ya," he says.

"We can't get in there."

"Not here, we gotta drive."

I walk on. "Not far," he calls after me. I turn and give him my disappointed look, as if I expect more from him. He points vaguely off toward the tree line. "Couple miles."

"No thank you. I mind my own business."

"Suit yourself."

The truth is I enjoy him. I find myself disappointed on days he isn't here. He's different from the neighborhood people, not an SUV driver, not a dad in suit, or a retiree in golf clothes. Besides, I do want to hear the story. So the next day I say, "I have car."

"Drive your car then, I'll show you where."

We shake hands. Meet at the gate. James Calo, 60 year-old paper boy in his newspaper van. Mrs. Lillian Beamons in my Buick Regal. Not sure why I go. As I said, I mind my own affairs, I don't go to neighborhood-watch meetings or keep track of sexual predators or join retirees for afternoon drinks and pinochle. My daughters say I'm antisocial, that I'd benefit from communal living with other "seniors"—the living dead if you ask me. There's an old man who wants to walk with me in the mornings but he can't keep up. I'm not going to wait for him. I'm not involved with daytime television, I don't care what Oprah says. I take afternoons naps, read in the evenings, retire early and fend off my children's phone calls and pleas to sell the house.

We pass through the gate in tandem, the pudgy guy waves. We drive a few blocks on a winding new road and turn into the shopping plaza where I buy my groceries and proceed around the Arby's Roast Beef and the Wal-Mart and come out on an alleyway obviously there before the plaza was built, then a dirt road through a stand of pines and palmettos, and finally into a rutted lane under a rusty metal arch sign that reads Circus City Trailer Park.

We bump down the lane leaving a wake of dust. The trailers are not the set-up-on-blocks type; these are mobile, pulled behind trucks. Rusty aerial apparatus hangs here and there, chrome bicycles, a trampoline covered with a tarp. This is a retirement village for people pushed out by the affluent sprawl of Sarasota. It's not the only one, but you have to know where to look, where the pines and palmettos have not been bulldozed, the snakes and rodents and retired troupers live in peace. My guide was correct; we haven't traveled more than a couple miles in a straight line from the neighborhood. But you can't go in a straight line because they've built circuitous streets and shopping centers all over the place. We pull up to a trailer. The name Hubert Faughpaw is carved into a wooden sign. An old man in a wheelchair is sitting in the shade of a carport. We climb out and Mr. Calo points at the old man and says: "That's him, Mr. Hube Faughpaw, the one and only."

"It would be polite to introduce us," I say in a low voice.

"Don't worry, he's stone deaf. A bit out of it too." He taps his index finger against his head. "Gotta be near a hundred." He goes down on one knee in front of the old man. "Mr. Hube," he yells. "It's Jimmy Calo. Your old trainmaster." There is no reaction from the old man. "Mr. Hube was never much for talking," Jimmy says. "Have a seat." He points to a folding lawn chair but I remain standing. A Mexican woman comes to the screened trailer door, looks at us and goes away. I hear her knocking about inside. Jimmy squats on his heels and blurts out, "They've found Mildred, Mr. Hube. They've gone and dug her up!"

The Mexican woman comes out of the trailer and shuffles down the wheelchair ramp carrying glasses of ice tea. "We hear on the news," she says. "He ain't said nothing."

Jimmy stands and takes a tea and hands me one. "Nothing to say I guess. Nothing we can do." The old man takes a deep breath and murmurs something. "What's that

Mr. Hube?" Jimmy yells. "It's me, your old trainmaster, Jimmy Calo!"

The old man lifts one finger. "Millie," he says.

"That's it Mr. Hube. Old Millie. They found her. What kinda shit storm is that gonna bring?" The old man says nothing else. He seems aware but not necessarily lucid, white foam gathers at the corners of his mouth. We stand sipping tea. The Mexican woman sits in the lawn chair. Jimmy says, "Mr. Hube, did we ever know her last name? What was Millie's last name?" The old man blinks rapidly, seems to point one runny eye at Jimmy. "What's that Mr. Hube?"

"Arkansas," the old man says.

"Arkansas! That's her name?" Jimmy turns to me and chuckles. "Old guy's a gas, ain't he? That's probably where they found her, out in the boonies, probably never knew her name. Mr. Hube took her in as child—I wasn't there then—a huge child. Sideshow stuff. It was common back then, we're talking way back, hicks out in the sticks where they—you know, cohabitate or whatever."

"Are you talking about inbreeding?"

"Yeah that."

"Folks come clutching wretched deformed offspring when the circus came to town, alligator-skin kids, Siamese twins, kids with flippers and fins, and the fatties." But Jimmy says Mildred was more than fat. She was big boned and tall. Even as a kid she must have weighed three or four hundred pounds. Before he has a chance to tell the whole story the Mexican woman recounts in rapid-fire English/Spanish a crisis having to do with her sister and the border police and she can't take care of Mr. Hube much longer because she has to travel to Mexico ASAP. I can't follow the whole story. It is clear circus people do not dump their old folks at assisted living. Jimmy says he'll see what he can do and starts edging toward the cars. "Time to go." We wave goodbye to Mr. Hube who sits like stone.

When I turn in at the gate Jimmy doesn't stop. He doesn't like the neighborhood after daylight. The Neighborhood Watch signs have eyeballs, the people glare at him—possibly he is a burglar or one of those pedophiles they fear. Someone who doesn't belong here. He honks and drives off leaving me to wonder what I'd just seen and heard and what exactly is buried across the street from my house. Inside I find phone messages from my daughters. The hysterical one in Boston: *"Mom! We heard someone was murdered!"* The stoic one in New York. *"What in hell's going on down there?"* The sunny one in California doesn't follow Florida news. People in California don't care about anyone outside their golden state—although she is most sincere in her invitation to *"Come live with us!"* But she also has the greatest number of rug rats and her husband is a classic "Dave's Not Here" character who drives me nuts. No, I'm happy where I am thank you. I don't call them back.

Curiosity gets the best of me, besides I have nothing to do, so I drive to the Ringling Museum in town. Ringling bought out most of their competition between 1929 and 1960; including the Hubert Faughpaw show. The museum is understaffed; no one knows anything about a fat lady on the old Faughpaw show. I find a binder of show programs with a foldout page dedicated to the sideshow, and one grainy photograph of a fat lady, nothing but a girl, billed as Shirley Temple's BIG sister. She had ringlets and a short baby-doll dress so the rolls of her white legs ballooned like gigantic sausage links. Where did they get patent-leather shoes that size? According to the caption "the fat lady" performed some sort of Good-Ship-Lollipop dance with a midget accordion player.

The next day, out walking early, Jimmy waits by the fence. He says the picture was surely Mildred when she first came on the show. By the time Jimmy joined the show as a train porter, just a teenager then, Millie was already too big to make it from the train to some of the show lots. He says, Mr. Hube had the carpenters build a stout buckboard and a bunch of the porters helped her settle into the thing and she was hauled over to the lot by a pair of mules. But as the years went by, Millie grew so big she couldn't leave the train. Couldn't move much at all, Jimmy says. Mr. Hube outfitted a boxcar for her, a ramp, and a huge bed of hay bales set into a frame of split logs. Part of Jimmy's job was to lug in the masses of food she consumed and cart off the tubs of her waste. She basically had to be fed like an elephant, cases of cabbages, whole roasted hogs, haunches of horse meat, wild turkeys, 55-gallon drums of water.

Women from the wardrobe department came once a week to bathe her and change the bedding. "Git up here boy," they'd say to Jimmy. "Haul up on that limb there."

It took all he had to lift one of her arms so they could scrub under it, then the other, the legs he hoisted onto his shoulders, staggering under the weight while they scrubbed and kneaded mounds of flesh then rinsed and sprinkled her all over with talcum powder. "It weren't like looking at a naked woman," he says.

Breasts were indistinguishable from rolls of slug-colored hills and valleys, creases like canyons tinged red where the talcum wore thin. Jimmy says she seemed in pain sometimes, or just plain miserable, but never complained about anything except cowboy novels. She was illiterate and liked to be read to and Mr. Hube said that was part of the job. On train runs or on one-night stands when it was impossible for Millie to make it to the lot, the porters took turns reading to her. She favored trashy romances and lesbian pulp paperbacks which were around then. She hated cowboy novels.

Jimmy worked on the show nineteen years, bumped up from porter to trainman, and finally trainmaster. The trainmaster job was as important as they come on a traveling show. The train was over a mile long and Jimmy was to see that nothing went wrong with it. If they couldn't get to the lots they couldn't setup and play which meant no money. Jimmy spent most of his time working with Mr. Hube, or arguing with railroad employees, or lecturing his crews. It took seventy men to operate, load, unload, and care for the train, and all of them were his responsibility. He didn't have time to pay attention to Millie. Still, as she got older and larger, she became part of his job because she became part of the train. Once, this he says he witnessed with his own eyes, on a rail scale that checks the weight of boxcars he calculated that Millie weighed close to 2000 pounds. "I swear to God," he says. "I done the math myself." Jimmy kept that information to himself, afraid if Hube found out he'd advertise it, raise a banner or something: World's Heaviest Woman! Too big to leave a Boxcar!

Even after she couldn't leave the train they came to see Millie, mostly kids poking around the railroad yards. If the train was parked in an urban area Jimmy would order the boxcar doors rolled back and town punks paid a nickel or a dime to climb the ramp and gawk at Millie sprawled across her hay-bale bed. Sounds brutal, but I understand Millie was the only person, animal, or thing on that show that didn't function to full capacity. There were no hangers on or slackers, everyone made the show go or Mr. Hube put them out. Except Millie. He kept her all her life, even if her world was what could be seen through boxcar doors.

"There were chances to be rid of her," Jimmy says. "Other show owners wanted to buy Millie. Mr. Hube always refused. Some church ladies showed up one time, wanted to take Millie to a home, said she needed treatment. Mr. Hube didn't run 'em off. He put it to Millie, I seen it myself," Jimmy says. "We tried to reason with her, but she threw a conniption fit, she weren't going nowhere. Mr. Hube threw up his hands. 'Fine,' he said. 'Let's get out of here.' We rolled in the night. Mr. Hube perverted the route so the church ladies couldn't find us."

Show routes traditionally follow warm weather, playing northern cities in summer and dropping south in the winter. Cold didn't bother Millie, she was well insulated, but in the summers she suffered mightily from the heat. Jimmy ordered her car constantly lined with 400-pound ice blocks. That's where unforeseen disaster struck. One night, on a mountainous run through West Virginia, the train rocking hard through tunnels and around tight turns, a few cars derailed. This wasn't unusual, show trains were designated to little used tertiary rails. It wasn't a bad derailing, none of the cars overturned, but they had to unload and jack a few cars back onto the tracks. Millie's car didn't derail so there was no reason for anyone to look in there, to check on her. Jimmy was busy all night and when they rolled on he slept. They woke him in Wheeling. They were stopped, unloading in progress. Two porters pounded on his door. "We got a problem," they said.

It was Millie. Jimmy hurried down to her car. They had little motor scooters to zip up and down alongside the train. She was dead when he got there, covered with blocks of melting ice. It was clear enough what happened. At the derailing the ice blocks, which were tied down and covered with canvas, broke loose, toppled over, pinning Millie to the bed and somehow killing her. They weren't sure how. Hypothermia or asphyxiation probably, or maybe she was crushed on impact which they hoped since it would have been most merciful. Millie had been on the show longer than anyone, she was such a force, sheer size alone, her presence both extraordinary and taken for granted—she was as much a part of the show as Mr. Hube himself. Jimmy says he doesn't recall telling him that day, or what he said. I press him on this. "How can you not remember?"

"I just don't. I 'member finding her, then standing in the car looking at her with Mr. Hube. I musta send someone to get him."

"What was his reaction?"

"In the car? Oh, he was pulling his hair out, he had

hair then, he kept stomping up and down and saying goddamn, goddamn—cuz see, there was no way to get her outta there."

When an elephant or horse died they were hacked up where they fell and fed to the cats, but Millie was well-liked on the show, beloved even, no one was willing to hack her apart. These were resourceful men, but they were in the middle of a season, they had towns to play, there was a route, a schedule. The choices were few. They decided to pack the car with more ice, close it up, and move on. The order came from Mr. Hube, but Jimmy was the one buying tons of ice that summer, every town having it delivered and packed into Millie's car by the porters. The whole thing made for a very uncomfortable season. Mr. Hube was frantic someone would find out he had a fat lady on ice. And what would happen then? Who knew the rules about such a thing?

No one found out. That November they rolled into winter quarters in Sarasota with a very cool Millie still on the show. "She'd lost a little weight," Jimmy says. He thinks this is funny and says it more than once.

The sun is up, the tile roofs steaming, SUVs rolling, kids waiting at bus stops, the newspapers are on the lawns. Through the chain link fence I see the mound of dirt and the plastic tarp covering the hole where they found her. "I gotta get on," Jimmy says.

"Whoa, wait, what exactly transpired in winter quarters?"

"What?"

"What'd you do with her?"

"Well, winter quarters," he throws his arms out in an expansive gesture, sneering at the streets and houses, "we're standing in it!"

The Faughpaw property, where this neighborhood sits now, was 1800 acres with rail access. The entire train rolled inside and the gate locked. Winter quarters was, as Jimmy says, their place. Remote, private, where they relaxed free of the public they relied on and reviled. It was the only time they were truly alone and they knew whatever had to be done with Millie had to be done there—here. What's clear now, listening to Jimmy, is that Mr. Hubert Faughpaw was a decisive man. He was absolute in his orders and he wasn't questioned nor known to second guess a decision. But with Millie he was vexed. She'd been with him all her life, fed and cared for. He would not, or could not, cut this woman up. They talked about expanding the boxcar doors with a torch, build a wider ramp, have the elephants pull her out. But then what? What mortuary could handle such a thing? What cemetery would give up a half-dozen adjoining burial plots? Who would pay for it? And what about the months spent on ice?

"Bury the car," Jimmy says. "That's what Mr. Hube said. I remember the day he said it. I was shitfaced—we was all shitfaced in winter quarters—and I couldn't get a handle on what he was telling me. The whole car? I kept saying? The whole car? That's what Mr. Hube said. 'Get the men digging, the car is where she lived, let her stay there.'"

In retrospect it seems fitting. This was circus ground after all, owned by the Faughpaw family since the turn of the century. Jimmy ordered Millie's car detached and pushed to the end of the rail spur where the car-stop was removed and the ties dug out from under the rails. The hole was dug precisely at the end of the line. They had a crude diesel-powered digger then; still, he says, the hole took two days to dig. They dug it with a gradual incline at the rail end so the car could be eased into the hole. The bull hands harnessed the elephants and they walked alongside the hole pulling the car in. The steel wheels sunk deep into the sand and there it sat with a 2000 pound woman in it. "There weren't no formal ceremony," Jimmy says. "Mr. Hube come out and watched the hole filled with dirt and packed down and later we built a tool shed on top of it."

That's the story news people are looking for. No one will tell them. I don't know how many around here know this story anymore, a few for sure, those that dug that day, and watched Millie put to final rest. Final until now.

The controversy dies down. The reporters find other stories to interest the public. The contractors find people to sue. The neighbors lament property values. The curator of the Ringling Museum offers to take Millie as an exhibit but only if someone pays for excavation. The mayor of Sarasota whines and complains, he is trying to attract money people to his expanding county and stimulate the local economy, he is overheard muttering "Goddamn circus freaks."

One morning, after my walk, after Jimmy has gone back out on the road, after the right people are paid off apparently, two cement-mixer trucks roll up and fill the boxcar hole, Millie and all, with concrete and when it's dry it is covered over with dirt and the police ribbon taken down and the construction resumes and the neighborhood goes back to normal. Sort of. Curving black asphalt streets are put down and nursery palms stabbed in along the sidewalks, lots are laid out, houses built, McMansions I hear them called, fertilized lawns and manicured bushes. Fresh-faced couples come from the snow states to buy and call this home. No marker or memorial is raised, nobody can say for sure then exactly where Millie is.

I know where she is. She is in a place where new neighbors meet old. Mornings after walking I drive over to check on Mr. Hube. The Mexican woman is gone and I make sure he eats and has clean clothes and bedding. I push him up and down the wheelchair ramp. As company he doesn't rival Jimmy that's for sure, not a talker, he spends most of his time in deep nod. But Jimmy will be back in the fall and I'll keep Mr. Hube until then.

My children get their wish. I sell the house. Recession or no this is still a sought-after neighborhood—not by me. I sell the house furniture and all to a couple from Chicago. They are thrilled. My husband, a believer in large life insurance policies, always said he'd die before me and so it is. I take a few clothes and my Buick and move into Mr. Hube's trailer. I buy a cell phone and monitor my calls. I have no address, no bills, no worries. I get social security checks at a P.O. Box. No one save Jimmy knows where I am. The weather goes hot, the trailer park quiet and steamy. In the mornings I walk the dirt road among the pines and palmettos and await the return of my sixty-year-old paperboy.

Turns out I sold the house just in time. Prices fall after the neighborhood expansion is finished and strange things start to happen. Sinkholes drop out of brand new streets, houses settle badly, cracks open in walls overnight, ceilings droop, mysterious molds appear, some say they smell popcorn in their basements. There are rumors, things under the surface, things manmade and not, things grown over and known by none who live on macadam drives with cracking swimming pools and Jacuzzi tubs listing on sinking cedar decks. At the end of streets rusted rail ends break through the surface, reaching like tentacles, snapped off and dangerous, old tent poles notched and tied with cables, iron wagon rims, wooden stakes topped with steel rings, coils of rope cocooned in spider webbing and the sucked dry shells of the fed upon, the remains of a galvanized tool shed, all packed and preserved underground in the sand and limestone as if some unnatural disaster descended onto this place rendering life scattered and frozen in a moment.

But that's not what happened here. Those who lived here were driven out by a hoard descending from the north like a tidal wave of time and money pushing them to land as yet unwanted—that will change too. So they left one of their own. It's not that they forgot Millie when the Faughpaw show closed. There was simply no way to take her. So Millie lives with the new people now, among townies from up north, among strangers, she keeps her eye on them. She is the gawker now. Grinning from her refuge, a bloodless skull with teeth like flagstones, ringlets a mile long, a bile system holding the whole world. Step right up folks; walk among the displaced critters and ghosts, follow the waves underfoot, the ground unnaturally soft here, hard beyond reason there, grass dying in yellow clumps, unexplained bald spots, circular depressions like astrological signposts. Just who is stranger here? The alligator boy with scales for skin, the flipper and fin kids, the inside-out man with gut-sacked organs gurgling and farting on the outside of his body, the Siamese twins, the androgynous dwarf, the albino mongoloid—this is their neighborhood.

Breathing

The ambulance came at midnight in the middle of the week, the alarm clock on the nightstand glowing in the dark, the light beams coming up through the window and circling on the ceiling over our bed. My wife, Mary, propped on one elbow, separated the Venetian blind slats with her fingers and peered out. There was no siren so I figured it was the electric company. All winter we'd had power trouble along the waterfront. "What now?" I said. There was always something downtown.

After spending a last Christmas in the old house in North Charleston where our boys had grown—two in college, one married up north—Mary and I, alone again after thirty years, didn't need a big place and purchased this townhouse on the water. For three months we've lived with the wind pounding the shutters battened over triple-paned safety glass. These places were built to resist, to stand up to, another Hurricane Hugo. I don't know that they would but that's what the city insisted, the contractor proclaimed, the realtor stressed: "You'll be safe here," the realtor said. "This neighborhood won't be leveled again."

We didn't feel safe. Mary was uncomfortable those first few months, wearing sweaters inside and hugging herself. She was used to an oil burner. These places had electric heat that tinged, took a long time to get hot, and gave me sinus trouble. We woke at night to unfamiliar noises, the water crashing, the wind pounding the walls. We'd been in the old house twenty-five years and had settled along with its familiar creaks and groans. By April it was warm downtown and we pushed back the shutters in the townhouse and opened the windows.

Outside, the ambulance engine idled at some insanely high rpm. I rose and went into the bathroom. Mary didn't say anything. She was sleepy, propped up, peering out, squinting and breathing hard.

Over the toilet was a round window that didn't open. Standing there peeing, I saw the ambulance backed into the clean cement driveway of the place next door. Men in white coats ran into the house pushing a stretcher on wheels. The red bubble on top of the vehicle spun and bounced light all over the neighborhood. There are no yards down here; the land too valuable for yards. Driveways and low hedges separate the townhouses along the water. I went back to bed. "Ambulance," I said.

Mary got up to use the bathroom and didn't come back. I was tired and wanted to sleep. We both had to work in the morning. There was nothing to see. I figured the guy next door had a heart attack. Joe Henderson, younger than me, but overweight, and always with a cigarette in his hand. Across the hedge we bragged about our vehicles, our investments, we compared notes on the construction of these townhouses. "Insurance bought ours," Joe told me. Before Hugo they had a nice little house down here. A family home, garage, good size lawn. In 1989 Hugo forced evacuation; they came back to nothing. "Looked like an atomic bomb went off down here," Joe said. He was short and barrel-chested; the right shape for a heart attack, and always waving the cigarette around when we talked over the hedge. His wife smoked too, and they had a son at home. A teenager. Maybe the kid overdosed on drugs. Nah, he's not the type. It was a heart attack. What else could it be? In any case I wasn't going over there. I didn't know them that well. But Mary's absence made it hard for me to fall back to sleep.

She worked full time managing an auction house on King Street. They bought out estates and held private sales. High-class stuff. Sealed bids only. Mary is in charge of acquisitions. I've tried to get her to stop, she doesn't need the job, but she enjoys her work even if it's stressful having to assess the worth of things, guessing what will hold value and what will turn to junk. I own a building restoration company, which after twenty years steadfastly refuses to run itself. We both work hard, and there is little reason for it. We don't need the money. I paid the kids college bills out of pocket; we own new vehicles, dine out, and drink expensive wine. The old house in North Charleston brought ten times what we paid for it 25 years ago, and while the new townhouse was costly, it comes with little monthly overhead. There is no lawn to cut, no gutters to paint, no shingles to replace. Living downtown is easy and if it wasn't for our jobs we'd be free and clear with our time.

I got up and went downstairs. "Mary?" She wasn't in

the house. I looked out the window at the neighbor's place all lit up. People in the street. The house on the other side of ours is full of tall Russian girls. A fact the realtor had tried to conceal. She didn't want us to know the College of Charleston owned the place to provide housing for scholarship basketball players. The girls use the driveway to pound out intricate basketball patterns. They have one of those portable hoops with a weighted base and rubber tires on it. They get into configurations, run fast and furious routines with three or four balls pounding on the pavement.

    I went through the kitchen and down to the carport. We live above our cars here in case of flooding. During Hugo this whole area was under seven feet of water. Mary stood in her bathrobe at the end of our driveway. She held the robe closed under her chin. I walked along the hedge wearing PJ-bottoms, a T-shirt, and a pair of slippers I'd received from the kids for father's day. The sky was clear and the stars clustered and sparkled. The ambulance engine roared over the breeze and the sound of the water. It was invigorating to be standing outside in our nightclothes. I put my arms around Mary from behind and she stuffed her hands into the pockets of her robe and rested her head back against my chest and I pressed my nose to her hair. "Heart attack?" I said.

    "Maybe," she said.

    A police car showed up and blocked the street, bright headlights, the bar on top popping red, white, and blue flashes.

    The Russian girls stood barefoot in their driveway. Six Slavic goddesses in wild bed hair and sleeping gear: gym shorts and long tank tops with numbers on them. An exotic collective of wide flat faces, flared nostrils, eyes round and almond-shaped. A group of giantesses with acres of taut skin, arms that wrapped clear around to their backbones, and remarkable Russian basketball feet.

The paramedics emerged from Joe's house rolling the stretcher. We saw Joe sitting up with his shirt off and his chest crisscrossed with white tape. He had one of those clear plastic masks on his surprised face.

"God," Mary said.

"Oxygen," I said.

We watched him load into the ambulance. Mary flinched at the vacuum slam of the heavy door, and the ambulance pulled out, a world of light moving down the dark street toward the hospital not more than a mile away. The cop followed, and we waited long enough to see Joe's wife back out of their driveway in her car. "Poor woman," Mary said. When her taillights blinked away, we turned and went inside. What else could we do?

In the morning I awoke abruptly to the thwack and wallop of basketballs hitting cement, the Russian girls pounding out their routine. I went down to the carport in my robe to get the newspaper. I'd slept poorly, seeing those flat pale basketball feet all night. Now they were firmly encased in flashy basketball footwear. The girls bucked and pivoted one against another; bumping and pushing, fair hair pinned and pony tailed, sweat flying and the sun not even above the horizon yet. I heard a shout and a ball came over the hedge and bounced into my carport. I tossed it back to them. The ball was hard as a rock.

The slap and rap of their game rang upward through my tall narrow house, four stories if you count the attic and the carport level. There is storage room down there, a barbeque grill still in the box, a garden hose, and the recycling bins. Everything brand new. From our old house we hadn't even brought the furniture. It was well used and didn't suit this place, Mary said. We bought modern airy stuff—everything white leather, glass, and chrome. The kitchen floor rattled while I made coffee and spread the paper out on the table. Maybe there would be something about our neighbor: Man next door has heart attack, or whatever. "They don't put stuff like that in newspapers," Mary said, when she came down dressed for work.

Weekday mornings she rose at 6:30, went into her bathroom, and emerged at seven preened and primed for the day. Pressed slacks, silk blouse, a blazer, sensible shoes, exactly the right touch of makeup and hair spray. Reading glasses on a gold chain around her neck. She has her hair, speckled with gray, cut short now. "Low maintenance," she says. Mary is still smart looking at 52, turning heads on King Street, still turning mine after thirty years of marriage. This morning though, she is puffy-faced and cranky. "I didn't sleep well."

"I know."

"Damn ambulance."

We heard Joe's wife come home about five a.m. and drive out again an hour later. Over coffee Mary called her machine and left a message. "If there's anything we can do...."

"Maybe you should cook a casserole," I said.

"Casserole!"

"The kid might eat it."

"Ridiculous."

"That's what people do I think."

"I'm going to work." She looped her purse strap over her shoulder and went down to the carport carrying her brushed steel Starbucks coffee mug that fit tightly into the depression between the seats of her SUV. I followed and kissed her goodbye and watched her drive off. We were both tired. The Russian girls still bounded up and down, bounced through their rigmarole. The beating basketballs shook the coffee in my cup. Made my teeth hurt. Every morning after hammering the cement until my house vibrated, the house that would supposedly stand up to Hugo II, the girls took off running down the street. They ran down Lockwood, up Wentworth, to the College of Charleston, presumably to their day of classes and basketball and more basketball. A torrent of indomitable Russian girls running into next week, striding into the future on legs I'd climb to the apex if I had the heart for it. Man Has Heart Attack While Climbing Tall Russian Girl, or whatever.

Joe's house looked hollow and empty, the wife's car missing, and the newspaper lying in their driveway. I went around the hedge to retrieve the paper and threw it onto the passenger seat of my Mercedes sedan. No point having the paper lay there advertising the fact that things had gone amiss. I went inside, took a shower, stood dripping at my desk and called the office. Most of my job involved meeting clients, considering new jobs, checking city codes, and working up estimates. We were restoration specialists, working on the old homes on which the city imposed a maze of ordinances. You couldn't just build an addition or paint your house without permission. I had to know the rules and regulations and figure out how to deal with them while keeping clients happy. That morning I went to a new job on Beaufain, a house so large the owner had spent five years painting it and the place was still a mess. Patchwork and peeling. The bushes and windows all dappled with paint. Ladders, drop cloths, empty paint cans and dead brushes everywhere. The man had inherited the house and was trying to econo-paint it by hiring old hippies in vans, lowland hicks in pickups. I told him my crew could wrap it up inside of a month for twelve thousand dollars. The figure put him on the verge of tears. "This house is pre-Civil War," he said, "it withstood Hugo."

"Restoration means putting back what is gone, extending life," I told the man. "That doesn't come cheap."

The man looked horrified. I felt sorry for him but there was nothing I could do. The old house had cracked bricks; the center roof beam of the carriage house was bowed. I left the owner to decide and drove around to jobs-in-progress. A clay tile roof on Broad, window replacement on Stuart, attic insulation on the Battery. Midmorning I was exhausted and stopped at Starbucks for coffee. I saw the College of Charleston basketball schedule, a stack of little cards with a calendar on the back, and slipped one into my shirt pocket. Maybe I'll purchase two tickets. Sit with Mary on Saturday night, a sweater slung over her back, eating junk food and dinking Coke like kids. On weekends Mary liked to sleep while I got up early, before the Russian girls even, and walked down Barre to the bakery. I'd carry back two capped coffees in a cardboard carton and a paper bag rolled at the top with two bagels still hot from the oven.

We have lunch together every weekday unless one of us is dining with a client. We eat at Del Veccios, my favorite place for loud heavy food, or have lighter fare someplace Mary likes. We drink wine or iced tea, depending on what we have to do in the afternoon. If we have wine we sometimes go home for a nap. Making love in places other than our bedroom, the kitchen, the bathtub, the car, has been thwarted ostensibly by Mary's bad back. "I can't be twisted into strange positions," she says. But maybe we've just grown too haughty to bear the embarrassment and coarseness of older people having sex in young places. After thirty years Mary knew everything I knew, everything I'd done, she'd heard all my funny stories, my morning farting, loud belching after lunch. The dollops of charm allotted to me were long dispensed and worn off for her, but we were still inseparable, incapable of imagining life without each other.

That day we had iced tea. "What are you doing this afternoon?" Mary asked me.

I was thinking of going to basketball practice at the College of Charleston but I didn't say that. "I have an appointment to look at a sailboat," I said.

"Not again," she said.

"Just looking," I said.

Our townhouse faced the marina. If we had a boat we could see it from the tiny deck that stuck out from our living room. *The Veranda*, the realtor called it. All the townhouses have the same little screened appendages: decks, porches, balconies, whatever. First thing to go when a hurricane hits.

"I'm thinking of the future," I said.

"I can't see us on a sailboat," she said.

Mary had dark circles under her eyes. "You feeling okay?" I asked.

"I can't even swim," she said.

"You should learn, be good for your back."

After lunch we walked down King Street. In the window of a travel agency was a replica of a giant white cruise ship, the QE2, or whatever. Mary pointed at it. "That's about our speed," she said.

In front of the auction house we kissed goodbye and I drove down Calhoun toward the marina. Maybe a cabin cruiser, I thought. Too much wind on sailboat. Joe's newspaper was still on the seat and I had to pass hospital to get to the marina so I pulled in. I figured it was the neighborly thing to do.

"Joe Henderson," I said to the desk nurse. "Heart attack."

"Joseph P. Henderson," she said, directing me to the correct room.

His skin was pasty white and he had an IV in his arm. A game show played on TV. There was a chair for visitors but I didn't sit. "How you doing?" I said.

"Oh," he said. "No one seems to know."

"Well, doctors."

"Yeah."

I carried his newspaper but there was one on the chair along with some magazines so I kept it folded under my arm. It wasn't like talking to him over the hedge. Joe seemed embarrassed about lying in bed since there didn't seem to be anything wrong with him. Turned out not to have been a heart attack.

"They don't know what happened," he said. "I was just sitting there, reading a Time magazine, my wife and kid already in bed. I sat there reading and falling asleep when suddenly I couldn't breathe."

"No," I said.

"Yeah," he said.

"No cigarette or anything?"

"No, no nothing, I just couldn't breathe. I got up and went outside. Figured some fresh air might get the blood moving. But it didn't help," he said. "I panicked. Went inside for my keys. Thought I might drive to the hospital."

"You should have banged on my door," I said. Mary and I slept while he stood in his driveway below our bedroom trying to absorb oxygen at any cost, through his skin, his brain, ingest it into his blood through sheer force of will, choking to death and begging God for air, more time, anything.

"I didn't know what I was doing," he said. "I thought I was in the eye of a hurricane."

"I've heard that," I said, "air is sucked from the eye, people at the true center suffocate."

"Worse feeling in the world," he said, "I just waited to black out."

"Then what happened?"

"I ended up in my car, started it, and switched on the air full blast."

I pictured him with his forehead pressed to the padded dash of his big white Cadillac, mouth open wide over the rectangular air vent.

"But it was no good," he said. "I figured they'd find me dead in the morning and think I committed suicide, so I went inside to wake my wife."

After the paramedics came and had him sitting up in the ambulance with the tape across his chest and the mask on his face he took clear breaths of oxygen and felt better. Halfway to the hospital he insisted he was fine and tried to talk the ambulance crew into turning around. "I'm okay now," he said, "take me back home."

The ambulance crew chuckled, "Not likely," one of them said, "we get paid to take you to the hospital."

"I'll write you a check," Joe said. "Really, I'm fine now."

The doctors at the hospital didn't think he was fine. "No more cigarettes," they said, and kept him there running tests, running up his insurance rates, writing on charts and scribbling prescriptions. The nurses brought pills and syrups and shots and bad food. When it was obvious they had no idea what was wrong with him, they let him go home.

A few months later, in the late days of August, when whatever breathable air there is in Charleston has been sucked down into the muck of the lowlands, it was the same routine at Joe's house. The ambulance came late at night, Mary propped on one elbow, a few months older, peering out through the blinds again, the lights circling on the ceiling again. "Like writing on the wall," I said.

Mary got up and put on her robe again. I went to take

a leak again and watched from the bathroom window. Once more we stood at the end of our driveway in our nightclothes, the wind blowing hard from the water, the Russian girls glowing and barefoot again. They'd been gone all summer, the mornings silent and lonely after Mary left for work. I'd stand naked and dripping from the shower longing for the pounding that gave a heartbeat to the neighborhood. I'd watch from the kitchen window, trying to catch Joe at the hedge retrieving his paper, grunting as he bent over and straightened up.

This time he was laid out flat. Strapped to the stretcher with white tape across his chest again and the oxygen mask on his face. His head slumped to one side. His cheek pressed to the white sheet. His lips blue and blubbery loose. His eyes bulging. "Trying to breathe again," I said.

Later we heard that he'd stopped.

This time Mary made the casserole.

Relatives came from out of town, filled his driveway with cars, parked in the street.

No one knew why Joe died, that was the scary thing. He just stopped breathing. We couldn't say "heart attack" then go through the next few weeks watching our eating habits, having cantaloupe for lunch instead of calzone, cutting down on bagels.

"Seems like there should be some reason," Mary said.

The newspaper said Joe was only 57. Four years younger than me. We vowed to take brisk walks around the neighborhood, planned to spend more time with the kids, maybe get that boat in the marina to watch over. I'd been thinking about a speedboat.

August droned into September. We got up early and went to work. A For Sale sign appeared on the house next door. Joe's kid went off to college. The poor woman was left alone. Hurricane season was upon us. We plotted the depressions coming across the Atlantic. What else could we do? In the evenings we'd set the portable TV outside on the veranda, the building warm from the sun beating on it all day, and we watched the water and stars, the mosquitoes dancing on the TV screen. The Russian girls would turn on their driveway light and pound the basketball, the sound ringing up through the dark house, blocking out the TV, driving the blood inside my head.

And when they stopped and went to bed, all together I imagined, and the blood settled down to my hands and feet, there was only the water and the sea breeze, potent and full, taking aim at how it was for us now. This is what we had come to, this what we had left after good times and bad, sickness and health. We held hands and sucked air gingerly, together, trying not to huff and puff, taking tiny breaths so as not to use up our quota.

LIVING AMONG STRANGERS

About the Author

Richard Schmitt is the author of *The Aerialist*, a novel (Harcourt, 2000), and has published fiction and nonfiction in *Arts & Letters, Cimarron Review, Gettysburg Review, Gulf Coast, North American Review, Puerto del Sol,* and other places. His story, "Leaving Venice, Florida," won 1st Prize in *The Mississippi Review* story contest. He has been anthologized in *New Stories of the South: The Year's Best 1999* and *The Best American Essays*, 2013.

Praises for *The Aerialist*:

Starred *Kirkus Review*: "...a fine debut novel, from a writer who has avoided the usual clichés and produced a work of genuine originality."

Starred *Publishers Weekly*: "Schmitt's debut is a beautifully polished tale....It has all the hallmarks of a potential word-of-mouth success."

Starred *Booklist*: "Is the traveling circus a microcosm of the extreme in the "real" world or a subculture that attracts escapists of too many roadblocks on the way to the American Dream?...The real story is not the spectacle of the circus itself but the life and drama behind the scenes."

Time Out New York: "Schmitt has made an impressive debut…loads the book with exotic details…deftly switching between a first person, macho, blue-collar voice and the lyrical third-person observations of an omniscient narrator.

Entertainment Weekly: "Cleverly turning the road-worn carny metaphor on its ear, Schmitt trains a follow spot on the perilous balancing act that is American ambition. This is the main attraction, but the sideshows—exquisite short-story cadenzas on the lives of the 'showfolks'—are even more dazzling."

Boston Globe: "It's hard to pinpoint a writer's ability to suck you in right from the start and keep you engrossed…but if this first novel is any indication, Schmitt has the gift."

Baltimore Sun: "It's the fiction writer's job to breathe life into old conventions, which is exactly what Richard Schmitt does…The Aerialist manages, with the savvy originally of a legendary old showfolk, to put an entire world inside a tent."

Salon.com: "The Aerialist, like its agile protagonist, has a way of pulling off complicated moves with seemingly effortless grace."

Ruminator Review: "The Aerialist…superb debut novel."

San Diego Union-Tribune: "The Aerialist"…more seductive than any first novel has a right to be."

Library Journal: "This is a tale of love and loss, of persistence, and of the value of learning what one really wants in life."